BLOOD FOR YOU

A LITERARY TRIBUTE TO GG ALLIN

EDITED BY
MP JOHNSON AND SAM RICHARD

WEIRDPUNK BOOKS
MINNEAPOLIS, MN

TRACKS

BONUS TRACKS

INTRODUCTION

MP Johnson and Sam Richard

Jesus Christ Allin, AKA GG, was born in 1956 to a father who was fucked up enough to name his kid after the son of God. GG got his nickname because his big brother, Merle, couldn't pronounce Jesus. As a teenager, GG's mom changed his name to Kevin Michael in hopes of making him normal. Too little, too late. GG went on to become the most notorious figure in the history of rock 'n' roll.

Yeah, there have been plenty of rockers who have done fucked up shit. Murderers. Nazis. Shitty people. But none have gotten the notoriety of GG Allin.

GG Allin is like a cartoon character – a horrible, obscene cartoon character with a rich history of fucked up behavior and a messiah complex, not to mention all the cum, shit, self abuse and abuse of others. He's got an army of obsessive fans that is balanced out by those who hate and deride him.

But the truth is, he was more than a cartoonish, one-dimensional, shit-spewing, face-bashing dunderhead. If all GG ever did was throw shit and bleed himself, he would have been forgotten soon after his death in 1993.

GG Allin was complicated.

Here was a guy who defied gender norms. He crossdressed. His high school yearbook photo is a picture of him looking like a conservative '70s mom. Yet at his shows, he oozed masculinity, picking fights with whoever came close to him.

He preached violence, but was almost always polite and respectful offstage. In some interviews he was soft spoken and thoughtful, while in others he was clearly putting on a show. He happily invited as many punches as he threw.

He didn't subscribe to straight or gay. He liked to suck cocks. He liked to fuck girls. He liked to have people pee in his mouth. He masturbated a lot.

He kept threatening to kill himself, yet he poured every ounce of himself into living his life to the fullest and doing it his way. He was committed to his art. Over the course of his life, he made numerous recordings, overcoming lack of money, lack of consistent collaborators, lack of anything even close to record label support. His recorded output ranges from catchy as hell songs like "I Wanna Fuck Myself" to sinister dirges like "Snakeman's Dance."

He was unrepentant about everything he did.

He was on a mission.

And it ended too soon.

That's where this book comes in. This book isn't really a tribute. Not really. It's not meant to aggrandize the man or apologize for the shit he did in his life. It's designed to put this character that had no place in the real world into worlds where he makes sense, and maybe to make sense out of who he was.

You don't need to love GG Allin to like these stories by some of the most insane authors working in underground fiction today. You don't even need to like him. Fuck, you can hate him, but that doesn't take away the fact that he was meant to fight a werewolf, devour the sin of the world, or prevent the apocalypse by piloting a spaceship to mankind's last functioning space station.

In these pages, GG is not tethered by the rules of polite society. He is free to do what he pleases. This is GG Allin's blood for you.

KENTUCKY FRIED CHRIST

Andrew Wayne Adams

Jesus Christ, this version of him, slid greasily into the world on August 29, 1956, a Virgo, and right away began his crusade of transgression, pissing and shitting on the doctors, nurses, and Magi there assembled for such an ahistoric whelping. He was an alien descended into a clay vessel, into a body like raw twists of dough, streaked with sludge the color of rust, and he was the happiest he'd ever be, crying and shitting and at the center.

In later life he would reattain to this feeling as often as possible, daily if he could, nightly, enacting his ecstatic formulae on stage with whatever rock and roll band he'd summoned to him for a time, or venturing into a beatific coma in back of a Greyhound bus as America spun dumbly past, or receiving a turd into his mouth from a syphilitic necrophile in the living room of an endless birthday party. Whatever the rite, it all circled back, really, to that first hour on earth, his arrival as a pure pellet of energy, wailing and retching and wholly himself, releasing his meconium (that infant dung like opium tar) from a sphincter fated as portal for God—singing, bleeding, weird, to where those assembled even forgave him for it, so innocent he was. Like just another babe, that was him, but for a simple sacred corridor in his mind: a passageway into risk and spirit.

This way, this path, would one day lead him onto *Geraldo*. It would lead him onto *The Jerry Springer Show* and into jail in Michigan and (in the form of a polycarbonate disc) into the teenaged hands of the present author (who, though no longer teenaged, still has hands) and various others all gone on to grinding ends. It would lead him to the Cook County Fair in 1977, there to play a show with his band the Jabbers (a slot obtained through some minor deception) and to meet the agent of his awakening (a meeting known of beforehand by

God alone; an awakening to fate, time, space, self, etc). And to get fucked up.

His set with the Jabbers lasted not long. It began with: "My name's GG Allin," for that was his human title, "and these are the Jabbers," whose bass player—GG's brother, Merle—had some feces in his mustache, "and this song's called 'I Wanna Fuck Your Brains Out'—cuz I do, I do, I got some AIDS here I wanna give you, I do, especially you, you old sow." It ended with a man with a clipboard rushing out a second later and grabbing GG's shoulder and waving the clipboard and using the word "police" and getting the clipboard smashed over his head by GG while the Jabbers crunched into their first chord, an E5, which was actually not the right chord, oh well, and the "old sow" in the audience, an elementary school teacher of thirty years, gasped and shook as her body got hot with anger, hot as well with the secret desire for GG to fuck her brains out and give her AIDS and smash a beer bottle across her face, and another man (without a clipboard in his hand but one in his mind) rushed to cut the power so that the shrill and shitty E5 vanished dryly after half a second, thus concluding GG Allin and the Jabbers' imprudent set at the Cook County Fair.

GG congratulated his bandmates on their new record time for getting kicked off stage. The song was a recent one he'd written, rawer and more direct than his usual shit, and he rather liked the reaction it'd gotten. Here, he thought, might lie a direction worth pursuing further. It certainly came naturally. He could easily write a hundred such songs, while drunk. Songs even worse—worse, which meant better. Already he was thinking of ones called "Suck My Ass It Smells" and "I Kill Everything I Fuck" and something about cunts.

Grabbing his acoustic guitar and a bottle of Jack Daniel's, GG snuck off into the diffuse churn of the fairgrounds. The Jabbers were moving on in the morning but he didn't bother telling them where he was going, where he'd be come dawn, for he himself knew not these details. Merle would find him. What GG and his brother understood, that the others did not, was that Merle's mustache acted as a kind of tracking device, its stiff bristles like antennae tuned to GG's whereabouts. All it needed to work was to have some form of bodily fluid from GG in it, which it always did.

A sign for an old-timey freak show caught his eye—the hermaphroditic midget with rabies and low self-esteem sounded like a thing he'd like to see, and fuck—but he kept on past, heading for a beer garden he'd seen earlier where he knew there was an open mic. Despite his pleasure at how things went with the Jabbers, he still had a hankering to actually, you know, play music.

When he got to the place there was a mongoloid at the mic. GG took a seat and let him finish, swigging from his bottle of JD with one hand while holding the neck of his guitar with the other, fingers absently forming a C. He settled back and stared out over the darkly wheeling distraction of the fairgrounds and he thought of the clown—the fat clown with the triangles around his eyes, triangles like sharp blue trowels, and a big watermelon slice of a mouth. He had seen the clown twice that day—just now on his way to the beer garden, and earlier that afternoon when the Jabbers first got in—and each time he felt a jolt, as if come against a shard of some outer world wedged here in dull reality. The clown had been posted outside the pisser, installed like a palace guard, handing out balloons to the men who went inside, and he made eye contact with GG each time GG passed... seemed to make eye contact with *everything*...

The mongoloid finished. GG took the mic and sang a Hank Williams song. Then he sang a tune of his own, then a Patsy Cline song, then another of his own. Some people clapped and GG was all right with that as long as they were happy and not just liars.

One of the people clapping was the clown. He stood in back of the beer garden, under a tree, his cluster of balloons grazing the low branches, and clapped with white-gloved hands. His grotesque pom-poms bounced. GG relinquished the mic to an elderly woman in dominatrix gear with safety pins through her exposed nipples. He walked back to where the clown stood clapping still and tipped the bottle of JD at him and said, "Drink?"

The clown stopped clapping and took the bottle in the hand not holding the balloons. "I liked that Hank Williams you played. What was the second one you did?" He drank.

"That was one of my own."

The clown handed the bottle back. "What's your name?"

"GG," said Jesus Christ, this version of him, for that was his human title. "GG Allin."

"I'm John. John Wayne. Oops," he giggled effeminately, "I mean, Pogo the Clown," grinning down at his billowy suit striped red and white. "But really my name is John, John Wayne, just like the Duke, that old macho Hollywood cowboy. That's right, I'm a real manly man," but he said it with a soft lisp. "I can trust you with my human title, I know, because there's something special about you."

"I just live how I want." GG poured Jack Daniel's in his eye. "You ever try smack?"

He had. A little later in life he'd start doing it all the time, but that wasn't yet. "Why? You got some, I might be interested in that."

"You'll hafta come with me if you want it. We can go to my restaurant and party."

GG decided to wait a minute before replying. He wasn't sure if he wanted to put himself in that situation. There was something about the clown he didn't like.

A screech of feedback drilled the air as the mic fell over, knocked down by the old lady with the safety pins through her nipples, who was whirling in a sudden scuffle. The row was with a man with a clipboard who had rushed in to stop her accordion act due to her exposed breasts and objectionable lyrics (she had just started into a song about the Holocaust). Half the crowd seemed to side with the man, the other half with the accordion player, and a third half with no one. Like a kind of limp war.

"There's something about you I don't like," GG told the

clown. He watched the tepid conflict over the open mic. The stalemate. "Let's get the fuck out of here."

They left, across the fairgrounds to the parking lot dark and vast, slipping through the mercurial tides of raw child, pickled teen, salted adult, through the cloying shroud of grease and the crow of prize alligators. Pogo the Clown drove a black Oldsmobile with sticky seats. GG kept his guitar up front with him and didn't wear no fucking seat belt. The clown steered with one hand while the other still held his clutch of balloons, those colorful globes choking the space inside the car.

In the time it took them to reduce the bottle of JD to a dribble, they drove a decade into the past, to 1966, it was, and from Illinois to Iowa, pulling up at last in front of a darkened KFC. GG, drunk, had no idea they'd driven so far through time and space. Even Merle wouldn't be able to find him here. He was alone with his fate. The Oldsmobile hissed as it cooled.

"This is my restaurant," said John Wayne. "I manage three of these. You like Kentucky Fried Chicken? I don't."

"I live on peanut butter sandwiches. I don't care."

They went inside. John Wayne kept the lights off but struck a match and transferred its flame to a candle. He said, "The dope's in the back. I'll go get it." And he stepped behind the counter and was gone, swallowed up by the maze of slumbering ovens, into the secret clockwork of the KFC.

There was an old-timey jukebox in one corner. GG went over and switched it on. He looked at the selection and found a David Allan Coe song he wanted to hear. The machine asked for a quarter, so GG walked over to the cash register, hit some buttons on it, but the cash drawer wouldn't open. Well, the cash probably wasn't in there anyway, not at night. He knew that. He was just drunk and enjoying it. Really wishing he could hear that song. And a couple of twenties might go well with that quarter. He smashed some more buttons.

The clown popped up from behind the counter, balloons first, still fucking holding those things, and looked at GG trying to rob him. "Stop that."

"Gimme a quarter for the jukebox, asshole."

"I got something better." And he unfolded the hand not holding the balloons, and in it was a baggie of heroin. "Come on... you first..."

They cooked up in a spoon encrusted with old coleslaw juice. From an oversized pocket the clown produced an empty balloon—one of the long slender ones used for sculpting animals—and gave it to GG, who tied off with it. Fat, greasy, giddy, the clown filled a syringe. "I can poke you, if you want. Let me do it."

GG looked at the needle, its payload of muddy quicksilver. Once the stuff hit his veins he'd go limp as a fuckdoll, he knew. His eyes traveled over the pom-poms on his host's billowy suit. The fat man shifted, and something clinked within one of his huge pockets. GG had been around the law enough to recognize the sound: handcuffs.

He thought: Pogo the Clown wants to kill me. Shoot me up, handcuff me, fuck me, strangle me. Man, that David Allan Coe song would go down well right now. He said: "You wanna kill me, I know. Shoot me up, handcuff me, fuck me, strangle me." GG always said what he thought, see. "Well, I still just want a quarter for the jukebox."

John Wayne lunged with the needle. As he did, he *finally* let go of his pack of balloons, which floated up to the ceiling and popped, each balloon releasing a scream as it burst. Around his eyes, the sharp blue diamonds of paint grew sharper, his jiggly face curdling into ropy arches—angry at being seen through, having some of the fun spoiled.

GG kicked the needle out of the clown's hand. "No one gets to kill me but me," he said. His movements were sloppy from all the whiskey.

John Wayne climbed on top of him and encircled his neck with white-gloved hands. The light of the single candle reached not far into the midnight depths of the KFC, and in its murk the murderer's eyes were little skulls. GG kicked, punched, tried to bite. He had long had a fascination with murder but never thought to be its victim himself; if anything, he would have expected to be on the other end of it, the doer and not the done-to. That was his way: to fuck life. Now life was fucking him.

Black dots attacked his vision, and his limbs were numbing from the tips inward, like lines getting erased. A jet of warm fluid hit his forehead, splashed down his face; the clown had regained the heroin syringe and was spraying him with it, as if with a squirting flower.

"I baptize you," said John.

At that, GG felt a bolt of spirit pierce him from a far-off star. Like a popped zit his mind shot out of time and space, and from the outside he could see it all: the full holy streak of his life, from his freak soul's genesis aboard a spaceship to its ultimate dissolution in a bacchanal of cosmic cum. On the cusp of death, just baptized, this was the vision he'd been forever hurtling toward, the awakening he'd been fated to. He gazed through the mineral clearness of his life, of all life, at the infinitely tentacled face of his author, himself.

He lived again his birth. He understood his mission upon this plane. He had a duty.

A duty to redeem and preserve the sacrament of rock and roll.

It was at that moment, as he learned of his nature and his fate, and as Pogo the Clown grew a wet spot on his baggy suit where an erection, oozing, stood up inside it—as Pogo tightened his grip, horny for the kill—it was then that GG discovered the divine talent inborn in him.

He shit his pants.

He had holes in his jeans from hard living, holes in his underwear, and those holes aligned to let the shit rocket out, and rocket out it did, a geyser of shit that struck the murderous clown in the torso with the force of a fire hose, knocking him away from GG. The clown rolled backward across the floor and slammed into the buffet, which tipped over, spilling its trays full of crispy chicken and mashed potatoes and baked beans, the food having been left out overnight for some reason, overnight and forever. Greasy bird pieces rained down onto John Wayne, and he rummaged through them for the breast he knew was full of razor blades, the breast he had so lovingly stuffed himself that no one had lucked into eating yet, damn them, oh well, and he found it and dug loose a razor and stood and faced GG, who turned and aimed his ass at the clown and let fly another volley of shit.

He had crapped himself before, obviously, while blackout drunk or on some drug, but this was different. He found that he could control it. Direct it like a weapon.

A rock and roll weapon.

The seat of his pants was now completely blown out. In the future (for he knew this weapon was to become a crucial part of the arsenal in his crusade) he would go pantsless or wear a jockstrap when entering the fray. Here necessity had forced him to ruin his jeans—or rather to finish ruining them... a good thing they had been so busted already... a certain logic to living always on the verge of expiry, in that it made it all the easier for a visceral pith to burst free... The sewage pissed out of him like a soup of coffee and opium tar, inundating John Wayne as if with sacred light.

"Stop that!" the clown managed to sputter.

GG did. "I'm outta here," he said. His voice was a rasp, brittle with coughs, from Pogo crushing his throat. "You can eat that fucking razor."

"Where you gonna go?" Pogo the Clown stared past him, out the black pane of the window, at the abyss beyond the KFC, and grinned. "You have no idea. What state is this? What year?"

He had to think through the whiskey. "Illinois, 1977. Who cares?"

"Try Iowa, 1966. We're at the crux of a space-time warp."

GG picked up his guitar where he'd left it leaning. "So how do I get back? I've got a tour to finish." And so much more.

"You don't get back." The clown kissed the razor with chicken grease still on it. "You're supposed to die here."

"Afraid not. No, I die on Halloween, 1993, on stage and by my own hand." For that was the end he had glimpsed in his vision. "After I terrorize America with my blood, cum, and feces."

"By your own hand, huh?" Pogo picked up the heroin syringe where it lay among some mashed potatoes. "We'll see about that." The syringe was empty from when he baptized GG. He stuck himself in the arm with it, through the silken sleeve of stripes red and white and spattered with shit and egg salad, and drew a dose of his blood into its belly. Then he put the needle to the razor, put it to the corner and drew the blade in like a drop of water—then bent to the spilled buffet and crabbed at thighs, biscuits, corn, saying, "This needle," sucking in the fat and the crumbs of everything, "This needle will be the end of us both." Finally the syringe was full with the astral magma, and the clown tiptoed forward with it pointed at GG.

GG raised his guitar as a weapon. "You know," he said, "there's something about you I like. But you should realize I'm not your victim. I'm no one's fucking victim. I think you and I could be friends, even. I don't know. I only know that I got shit to do."

"And what's that?"

"Put the danger back into rock and roll."

"Like me. I put the danger back into post-modern suburbia." He kept tiptoeing forward. "I guess we're alike, then. Two spores shook loose from Trickster."

"I'm about to shake your fucking skull loose, fatso."

"Fun!" said Pogo the Clown, and pounced.

GG had backed up to the jukebox. He still really wanted to hear that song. He sent a kick flying backward at the machine, and the thing started up, so that suddenly this KFC at the crux of deep-fried space-time was all ablare with the outlaw twang of country-western.

Pogo stabbed at GG with the needle, and GG swung at Pogo with the guitar, and the two weapons collided and annihilated each other with a flash that gave off a few ghosts. Pogo screamed and the crotch of his suit tore away as his penis (still hard from when he was strangling GG) ripped into the open, a demonic stiffy with its own will. The boner whipped its head around, the meatus flexed like a nostril. The glans was painted white with clown makeup.

GG laughed and John Wayne came at him and the clown penis jabbed like a cobra at GG's crotch and gnawed through the worn fabric instantly to where GG's dick was, and the demonic hard-on opened its meatus wide and gobbled up GG's penis like a lamprey eel eating an oily ladyfinger. Yet the devouring cock did not bite through the other, only held it in its throat, jacketing it, GG's dick stuffed like a sounding rod down Pogo's urethra. And thus they were joined, the two comedians, bridged at the groin. GG thought it maybe even felt a little good, and said so.

Then GG unhinged his jaw, like he now knew he could—one of the many powers his vision had awakened him to—and just as the clown had swallowed GG below, GG swallowed the clown above. The painted face slid greasily over his tongue as he sucked the man in, maw stretched huge to accommodate the fat cranium. He got the whole head in, dilated his jaws even wider to start on the shoulders. Meanwhile the clown's penis inhaled its food further, down to the base of GG's shaft and beyond, meatus expanding obscenely to ingurgitate the hanging scrote, breaking GG's pelvis forward so that it too went down the hungry urethra, thighs and belly sliding in.

And thus they proceeded, each eating the other, a kind of Ouroboros of course, collapsing to the filthy tile, until they were but a shriveled ring, an onion ring on the floor, threatening to wink out of existence completely, until a blast of wind from the jukebox, which still wailed its outlaw lament, sent the onion ring tumbling across the KFC, up over the counter and through a spiderweb and into the seething grease of a deep fryer that had been left on overnight for some reason, overnight and forever.

There, in the amniotic amber of hydrogenated oil, Jesus

Christ and John Wayne, together in the form of a frying onion ring, communed for a final eternal second. GG thanked the clown for trying to murder him: it was just the kind of initiatory rite he'd needed to wake the fuck up to the full import of his life. The clown thanked GG for hosing him with feces: it was just the kind of degrading frolic he'd needed to feel a glint of satiety. The two souls came to an understanding that they had much to learn from each other and would meet again on a different page of the universe.

Then the burning oil shook apart their structures, and the jukebox with its redneck scumfuc music started shooting solid bars of light from its display, streamers of neon fanning out like ribs, because this was a special jukebox with this one-time-only feature and *now* was the *one time.*

The girders of light unwove all that was solid, deconstructing the KFC and its contents, including the deep fryer with Jesus Christ's atomized soul in its crackling oil—unmaking the oil along with everything else, so that the oil *was* everything else, an ocean of golden unity: the oil was an acid pool on Venus; the oil was lube on an ancient stone dildo of Sumerian make; the oil was the whiskey in GG's brother's bottle as Merle drank while getting his dick sucked by an old dominatrix with a clipboard at the Cook County Fair, 1977.

GG—his soul one with the oil, and the oil one with the whiskey—shot up out of the bottle as a ghost. He entered Merle's mustache, where some of his own blood was caked from two days ago when Merle kissed his gashed forehead. His soul found his blood and built a body of it, a chemico-physical process similar to the dilation of seed into tree, and the body lay in the dirt next to a cigarette butt and a dropped slice of pizza and Merle's blowjob, writhing, naked as the day it was born because this *was* the day it was born, this day and every day. He was an alien descended into a clay vessel, into a body like raw twists of dough. He shat out a bright balloon. In his freshly struck brain he could still hear the song of that special jukebox, and knew the jukebox was him.

Merle looked at his magically materialized brother and muttered, "Fuck, I ain't drunk enough for this." So he swigged some more.

GG sat up. He was shivering cold in his nudity, defenseless under the starry sky, his body a temple cratered with the thousand comets of destiny. Taking the bottle from Merle, "I thought of some new songs," he said. The dominatrix going down on Merle had four, five pairs of tits, like a sow, plus a dick, and GG decided he'd go next. "Some new songs," he said again.

And the life to go with them.

THE GG EFFECT

Jeff Burk

Dr. Kevin Michael Allin was at the University of Cambridge on a residency, teaching theoretical mathematics, when he made a terrible discovery. It was early December and his classes were long over for the day. When he didn't have to deal with grading papers or writing lectures, he liked to tinker around on his various theorems on the classroom chalkboards. He found working out his long and complex equations on a chalkboard to be more mentally stimulating than a cramped notebook.

He stepped back from the board and stared at the numbers and symbols in horror. Mentally, he reviewed the process trying to find a mistake—there had to be a mistake.

But, no. He went over it three more times but there was not denying it. His math was correct.

Kevin sat at one of the front row desks, took off his glasses, and rubbed his shaved head in frustration, trying to process what he had discovered. He had no idea how much time had passed when Dr. Merle Allin—Kevin's brother and research assistant—entered the room.

Merle looked at him with some concern, and then at the chalkboards.

"Are you OK?" asked Merle.

Kevin tried to answer, but looking at his brother caused memories of their life to come rushing back. Memories of how far they had come from their parents' modest house in New Hampshire. All the wonderful machines they had invented. How hard they had worked to get here, running the world's foremost study in the abstract and theoretical sciences.

"Kevin," Merle said with growing concern. "Are you alright?"

"Yeah, yeah," said Kevin shaking his head, trying to clear the disturbing and unnerving thoughts clouding his brain.

"What's the matter?" asked Merle.

Kevin stood and waved at the chalkboards. "This."

"Is that your GG Formula?" asked Merle, stroking his bushy mustache and looking it over.

"Yes."

"Come on, Kevin. You know no one else can make sense of it."

The GG Formula was something Kevin had come up with when he was in graduate school for his first master. It stood for "General Guideline Formula." It was a masterpiece that earned him his first Nobel Prize. Kevin had figured out how to equate historical, political, and technological events into a numerical formula. This allowed him to anticipate the trends and demands of society. He could address needs before anyone knew anything was needed, and he could create new inventions before anyone else knew the direction the tech world was headed. He wrote a book about the formula—*A Simple Guide to Understanding Everything*—but no one could seem to get it to work.

It was groundbreaking. The things he created changed the course of all humanity. And he was never wrong.

"So what is it?" asked Merle. "You know, I really hate it when you pull this genius shit."

"It ends," said Kevin.

"What do you mean?"

"It just…ends."

"So you came to the end of the formula?"

"No. I came to the end of everything."

Merle looked over the hastily scratched chalk figures, but it was a meaningless gesture of trying to understand.

"To the end of everything?" said Merle. "Well that sounds just a tad bit overly dramatic. Maybe you just finally came to the end of *your* equation."

"No, it can't work like that. The formula should go on

for as long as events happen. For it to just—stop—it means nothing will continue to happen. It can only mean the end of all things. And all the variables point to just that happening—and we're already too late to do anything about it."

Merle cocked his eyebrow at his brother.

"Something's very, very wrong," said Kevin.

"OK, you sound like you've been working *way* too hard and long," said Merle while motioning to the door. "You got a long day tomorrow and you need to get some rest."

"No, no," said Kevin. "I *need* to stay here and keep working on this. There must be some way to change the outcome."

"Come on, you can worry about that when we get back," said Merle. "You don't want to make Tracy upset, do you?"

Kevin glanced over at mention of his wife's name. She was probably already upset. He'd barely been home that week and he still needed to pack for the three days they'd be spending in Sweden.

"OK…OK," Kevin weakly submitted.

Merle led him out of the classroom and flicked the light off.

"Just think," Merle said. "Maybe you're wrong."

The words hung in the air with thick trepidation.

💀💀💀

Kevin sat at the head banquet table in Stockholm, Sweden. The crowd was large and boisterous. Everyone was eating and drinking, celebrating his success. But Kevin felt no joy for his accomplishments. His chest had been tight with dread since his discovery.

That weekend he had received his fourth Nobel Prize, something no other human being had ever accomplished. He should have been celebrating his success, but he just couldn't shake the feeling of an impending disaster. He could tell that Tracy had noticed that something was off, but she hadn't said anything to him—most likely just chalking it up to his award-nerves.

He cut off a piece of pheasant and slowly chewed on the greasy game bird while looking around at those sitting by him. Tracy looked beautiful—decked out in Dolce and Gabbana for the prestigious event. Next to her were their two daughters, Nico and Ann. They were both eleven, born as twins. Their lives were still just starting, but they were already smart and outgoing. Beyond Kevin's numerous prizes, they were what gave him endless pride.

And then he wondered what would happen to them when it all ended and, whatever it would be, happened? Would it be quick? Would they be happy and laughing one moment and then, with no notice or sensation, be gone? Or would it be agonizing? Would they suffer…?

"Dr. Allin, a moment of your time, if you please."

Kevin turned to see an older man with no hair on his head but for a snow-white bushy mustached. He held out his hand with a large smile.

Kevin shook it. "How do you do?"

The man congratulated Kevin on his unrivaled accomplishments. He said he represented a group of men—very rich men. They would fund Kevin for whatever he wanted. He would be free to pursue any flight of intellectual fantasy he wished. All they wanted was a cut of the profit from whatever he created. The man explained, that would only be fair—as they would be giving him an unlimited budget with no time constraints.

"I'll think about it," said Kevin.

"That's all I ask for," said the man as he handed Kevin a card. "Take some time to enjoy yourself and consider the possibilities. After you're home and rested, give us a call."

The man stood up to leave, but paused as if something was on his mind. He turned back to Kevin.

"I believe we can do good things together, Dr. Allin," said the man with a jovial grin. "Big things," he said, and then was gone.

In the weeks after arriving home from the ceremony, Kevin could barely go through the motions of teaching his classes. His mind was constantly eager to return to studying his formula—which he did with every available moment. He barely ate and rarely slept; he was only dedicated to finding some sort of loophole or error.

But he found neither.

Once he had resigned himself that there was nothing he could do, he called the number on the card the man gave him. A quick chat and a very generous advance to his bank account proved that the stranger was not lying.

He told his wife about the new job he now had and lied that the obvious stress he had been under lately was from trying to decide on the position. It would involve a move back to the United States—New Mexico to be precise. At first Tracy and his daughters had objected, but when the financial matters—and glories—came up, Kevin was able to win them over.

He managed to work out that Merle would continue on as his assistant. So, they waited for the semester to end and then traveled back to their country of birth.

They had a large warehouse with a full staff for their studies. Kevin told them that they were working on creating the first stable transporter that could be used to instantly move large amounts of goods across the globe and, eventually, people.

But Kevin had only told Merle what they were really working on. A few years back a research team had created a large hadron collider for testing particle and high-energy psychics. While it was under construction, some in the press put forward the statistically unfounded theory that the machine could create a black hole on Earth and destroy everyone. Of course, that was a silly worry. The machine was designed in no such way and unlikely to suffer such catastrophic failure.

But Kevin and Merle's machine was designed to do exactly that.

Kevin could find no way out of the ending the GG Formula predicted—they were already too far into the events that set everything in motion. The only chance for all of humanity, perhaps all of reality, was for Kevin to go *outside* of reality. From there, maybe, if he was lucky, he could alter whatever set them down this dead-end path.

The machine was designed in such a way that a subject could stand in the exact spot where a black hole would form. It would completely envelope the subject at once and, in theory, expel them outside of our fourth dimensional space—outside of the constrictions of time. From there, Kevin could travel through time to right whatever was wrong.

At least, that was their idea.

Even though Merle knew what they were really working on, there was still one secret Kevin had hid from him.

They had been up late one night, drinking in the lab, reminiscing, when Merle asked a question.

"So, when you go through that thing, what happens to the rest of us?"

"What do you mean?"

"I mean, we're creating a black hole in a lab—which is a stupid enough idea on its own. That you're going to travel through to save humanity's future—which is even fucking stupider." Merle slurred that last part a bit. "So while you're through, what about everyone here? Will the hole suck us all in?"

"No, no," said Kevin. "It should only exist for the smallest fraction of an instant. One moment I'll be there and then I'll be gone—outside everything we know. Hopefully, I can fix it. And hopefully, I'll be back."

"And how do you think you're going to do that?"

"I'll figure it out."

Merle grunted and threw back another shot of whiskey.

Kevin stared down at his shot-glass and the amber liquid within. What he just said was all a lie. Anything could happen when they created that black hole. It *could* be extremely unstable and disappear instantly, taking him with it. But it was also just as likely to rapidly expand and suck the very Earth into it.

But the world was going to end anyway and there was nothing they could do about it. Isn't it better to risk everything for one chance to save everyone? Kevin thought of his daughters. This was his only chance, slim as it may be, to give them a future.

And there was no coming back—this was a suicide mission.

He took the shot and slammed the glass down.

There was nothing to worry about. He was never wrong.

💀💀💀

It didn't take them nearly as long as Kevin thought to finish the machine. Part of him wished it had taken longer. He had actually been working only a normal eight-hour day and then spending the rest of his time with Tracy and the kids every night—trying to enjoy what little he still had with them.

But the end of the GG Formula could happen at any moment, and he was lucky to beat its arrival.

The day it was to be turned on, Kevin and Merle sent the rest of the staff home for the afternoon. They didn't want anyone realizing what they had been constructing and shutting down the powering on process.

Kevin and Merle barely said anything to each other, both committed to the project and lost in their own thoughts of the implication.

Even while they did the final practice run, they were nothing but business.

When it was all set and ready to go, Kevin headed to his platform and Merle headed to the main control panel. Their paths crossed and they both stopped to look each other in the eyes. And then they hugged.

"Good luck, brother," said Merle.

"To you as well…brother," said Kevin.

And then they got in place.

"Ready?" asked Merle over the intercom. The main controls were in a small room that overlooked the machine. The room was shielded to protect the machine's operator from any radiation.

"Ready," confirmed Kevin.

Kevin could hear the flick of the on-switch. The machine hummed to life around him. It was a loop of garbage-can-thick metal tubes that ran in an oval the size of an Olympic track field. Leading from the main tubes were much smaller ones that ran into and through the walls surrounding him. On the other side of those walls were massive computer banks that would be performing all the complex equations and operations needed for their hacking of reality.

"Ignition in 5..." said Merle's voice over the intercom. There was a slight shake to those words.

Kevin's fists gripped tighter.

"4."

The overhead florescent lights glowed brighter.

"3."

The machine's tubes began to shake as if they came to life with a loud, whirling whine.

"2."

The lights grew brighter and brighter. One exploded and rained down shards of glass.

"1."

The machine shook harder and harder and whirled louder and louder.

"Igniting."

Kevin thought of his family.

More of the lights overloaded from the massive surge of energy coursing through the building. The machine rattled to the point that Kevin briefly wondered if it was going to shake itself apart.

And then there was a noise. It was overwhelming and shattered all his senses for its millisecond duration. In that time he heard every man, woman, child, dog, cat, cow, fish, bird, fly, beetle, bee, flower, tree, blade of grass, and all the rest of God's creations cry out at once.

But then they all went silent.

☠☠☠

Kevin had felt nothing. No sense of movement or force in any way on his body, but he was definitely somewhere else. He was surrounded by complete and total blackness. Not darkness, as he could see his own body with no difficulty, but just open blackness in every direction as far as he could see.

He stepped forward and his shoe landed with a loud *clunk*. He looked down to see that there was a floor like pure, polished obsidian that seemed to go on forever.

He took a few more steps forward and looked around. It was almost like being in an eternal sensory deprivation chamber.

Then he saw the light. It was just a tiny pinprick of pure white, but it stood out bright against the never-ending black. And the light began to get bigger. It grew to the size of a baseball, and then a car, and then a house, and then the entire horizon.

Soon it filled his vision. The brightness hurt his eyes, and some tiny back corner of his brain felt like it was being stabbed.

And then the light overtook him. There was a brief flash of warmth and then white went over and around him.

There was scenery speeding past him to his left and right. It was like he was on an invisible super-sonic train running under an eternal night. But, no, he wasn't feeling any movement—he remained perfect still. Only his surroundings were moving.

He walked to within a foot of objects flashing past and peered into them. There were flashes of color and depth. At times Kevin thought he saw brief glimpses of figurers—people—moving within the blur.

He moved back and waited for what he thought were just a few minutes—but there was really no way to be sure. The objects didn't show any sign of stopping.

He looked around, but nothing was changing and he didn't see anything new, just everything continuing to speed past. He looked back at the things hurtling by and considered his options.

He reached out until his fingers were just inches away. He breathed in deep and then pushed his arm forward.

There was a bright flash and then he was in the living room of his parents' house. Above the fireplace was his grandfather's cuckoo clock with the front corner chipped away. There was the faded brown couch. And his father's recliner with a coffee table next to it with the newspaper and ashtray.

His parents both died in a car accident when he was twenty-three and away studying. He hadn't been able to come home for the funeral due to tests. The house was sold shortly thereafter. Kevin hadn't seen the room since he closed the deal with the realtor and, quite frankly, hadn't thought about the house in the many years since.

Three figures shimmered into place. His father was sitting in his chair with a content smile and a whiskey. His mother came into place on the couch. She was leaning forward with pursed lips as if she was in the middle of saying something.

The third figure appeared next to her on the couch. It was a much younger Kevin—around eight or nine. He had his head in a comic book—*Tales to Astonish*.

All three figures were perfectly still and didn't breathe or blink. Kevin looked them over.

His plan had apparently worked to some degree. He was out of time in, currently, some preserved moment of his own past.

He continued to inspect the room. While this was intellectually fascinating, it wasn't helpful to his goal.

He came to the fireplace mantel, where the old wooden clock hung above. The mantle was decorated with various family mementoes from his parents' past. There was a framed picture of his mother's parents, a porcelain elephant, and various other knick-knacks. He picked up a framed picture of Merle and him—they couldn't have been more than four. They were sitting outside in the grass on a bright sunny day. They both had big, joyous smiles.

Kevin set the picture down and it *clinked* on the hard wooden mantel.

He turned around and all three frozen people now had their heads turned. They were staring at him. They didn't appear to have moved in any other way, but all three now had quizzical expressions and were looking at his exact spot.

Kevin slowly moved to the side and they didn't move or change.

Then Kevin realized they hadn't been looking at him. They had somehow heard him setting the picture down. This gave light to a new discovery—he could interact with what he saw and experienced here.

But being in his parents' old living room wasn't going to help anything.

There was a flash again, and then he was in his old bedroom. Kevin saw younger him, but older this time. Sixteen for sure. As soon as his senses took hold, Kevin remembered this specific day.

He was sitting on his bed reading a book he had checked out from the library, *The Origin of the Species* by Charles Darwin. If he could pinpoint one moment that sent him down his entire path of inventing and intellectual pursuits—it would be this. That book opened up a whole new world of mental exploration for him.

Another flash and he was in the ballroom from just a few months ago, receiving his fourth Nobel Prize. Like before in these out-of-time travels, all the people were frozen in place.

This was starting to get a bit frustrating. He wasn't here for some *Christmas Carol*-like journey into his own past. He had a mission.

Then another flash. He was standing in the ruins of some massive city. What used to be skyscrapers were now just smoldering empty husks. The streets were filled with broken concrete and twisted metal. Fires burned but the flames were still in the air, like a freeze-frame from a movie.

In front of him were two human corpses. Their clothing and skin had been completely burned away, leaving them red and black like overdone barbeque.

This was the end he predicted. The end of everything. But how did things get so bad, so fast? What could he possibly do to prevent it?

And then it hit him. He wasn't seeing an overview of his past. He was seeing the events that led to this. Somehow, he was the one responsible for the end of the world. All this death and destruction—it was because of *him*.

It was his influence on the world that led to this end. His GG Formula wasn't just accurately predicting what was coming next—he had been solving for the end.

It was all his fault.

Guilt and depression hit him, hard. His legs gave way and he fell to the ground. In his attempts to improve all of mankind, he had ruined it. He took everyone's future away. His family…

But then a new resolve hit. This is what he was here to prevent. He had a rare opportunity. This was no mere premonition of what was to come. He could still fix it.

There was a flash and he was in his old hometown library. He saw himself at the counter with a small stack of books. The frozen old librarian smiled at his sixteen year-old-self.

Kevin went over and looked through the books his younger-self was checking out. There, in the middle, was *The Origin of the Species*.

It's funny how the world works. We rarely realize how many little events must go just so, in order for us to get to the place where we currently reside. One little change to the past can alter someone's entire course and they never get there.

Kevin was very much aware of that precariousness.

He stuck *The Origin of the Species* on a shelf and grabbed another book at random. He looked down at it, *The War of the Worlds* by H.G. Wells. A fun little potboiler that he read later in his life. It was enjoyable, but these flights of fancy were never really his thing.

Kevin replaced *The War of the Worlds* in the middle of the stack. Without *The Origin of the Species,* he never would have had that inspiration, at that key point in his life, to pursue the sciences.

Now it was just a matter of where his life would go.

There was a flash and he found himself in another ball-room—not the same one from his Nobel receptions, but still ornately decorated and filled with people in fine suits and expensive dresses.

An older version of him was at the front table as he was receiving a Pulitzer Prize. He must have grown into a writer in this new timeline.

Kevin smirked. *Well, at least I'll still be good at something.*

A flash and he was back to standing in the ruined city. Nothing had changed.

What? he thought with indignation. He had changed the past, but yet he was still seeing a doomed future. This couldn't be right!

So he went back again. He changed it so he grew into a painter, a baseball player, and even a star ballerina. In each scenario, he saw himself becoming recognized for his achievements and then the same image of burning buildings and dead people.

No matter what he changed, his influence still damned everyone and everything.

Was there nothing he could do to change the future? Was this a futile mission?

He flashed back to his parents' living room when he was much younger. The first place he went to when he entered this strange plane of existence.

Kevin smiled sweetly at his mother and father. They had loved him so much and were so kind and caring. Little did they know that their little boy would grow up to be the cause of the apocalypse.

Then, he knew why this was the first stop on his journey. It wasn't the book that set him out on his course in life—it was *this* that prepared him so well for the future. His parents had raised him with support and guidance. He was so well equipped for whatever path he chose that he could *only* succeed.

That's what he had to change.

A flash and he saw a very young boy, no more than three, sitting on the floor of a log cabin. He knew this was his father. It was so strange to look at someone who helped create you, so young and so fragile. His father, as a baby, had an expression of pure joy and happiness. He was playing with a toy train on the floor.

Kevin picked up the toy.

It felt wrong. He didn't like taking a toy from a child, much less one that would one day later be so loving to him.

But the knowledge of what he had to do gnawed at his consciousness. While this would feel bad in the moment, it was for the good of everyone to come.

He threw the toy as hard as he could at a nearby window and, to his surprise, the glass shattered with a loud crash. It was the first noise and movement from something other than himself since he came here.

There was a flash and Kevin was still in the same room. His father, still as a baby, was sitting on the floor—mid-scream with tears frozen across his face. A man and woman stood over him. It must have been Kevin's grandparents, with stern looks on their faces, scolding the child.

Kevin traveled through his father's life. Changing as much as he could in little ways. Changing his tests from school to give him failing grades, destroying his paychecks, moving his possessions around to subtly shatter what he thought he knew of object permanence.

At this, he felt guilt. His actions were having cruel effects. Kevin did everything he could to make his father's life much more difficult in little ways. He knew from the way his father had told Kevin of his past that he prided himself on always being a hard worker and that the world had rewarded him for his toils with a beautiful home and family.

But now Kevin was changing his father's past so that every step of his life would be just a desperate attempt at survival. With no prospects for the future and a never-ending string of "bad luck," he would not be the same man who raised Kevin.

But then the guilt left and Kevin was resigned to his mission. This was bigger than him or his father.

And Kevin was back in the room with his much younger self. But everything was different. His younger self was sitting on the floor, mid-cry. He was not in the house he remembered from his youth, but in a log cabin just like the one he saw from his father's past. The place was dirty and in a state of disarray with crushed beer cans and cigarette butts littering the floor.

The biggest change was his father sitting in a chair in the corner. He no longer looked like the middle-class happy family man Kevin remembered. In his place was a man wearing stained and torn clothes. His hair was grown past his shoulders and frayed. His face was unshaved with days old patchy spots.

It was in his eyes that there was the biggest difference. These were not the soft and understanding eyes Kevin remembered. These were wild, like a caged animal longing for something weaker to let its guard down and venture too close. There was cruelty and insanity sparking.

Kevin shivered.

A flash and Kevin saw his sixteen-year-old self. He was not in his room reading, like he remembered doing most of that part of his youth. He was now on a street corner in what was obviously a very bad part of the city. His younger self was dressed in little more than rags and giving a baggie of something green to another kid on the corner.

Kevin moved closer and saw that he was giving marijuana to the other kid.

Great, I became a drug dealer.

Then another flash and Kevin saw himself as a young man. He knew it was him but there was little physically in common with what he viewed as himself. He was on stage at some dingy club singing in front of a band. He was dressed only in a jockstrap. His head was shaved and he had a mangy goatee. Blood was splattered over his body from open wounds on his chest and forehead.

The band backing him looked like the type of people Kevin would normally dismiss as "scum." Then he noticed Merle. He was playing a bass guitar and, just like Kevin, looked like a ruined shadow of his former self.

Oh Merle, I doomed us both.

A flash and he was in a cemetery. He was behind a tombstone that some degenerate wearing a patched-up and metal-studded leather jacket was pissing on.

Kevin didn't need to look at the monument. He knew this was his new future. To be honored by some punk pissing on his eternal resting spot.

A flash and he was in some city from out of his wildest dreams. There were people everywhere wearing strange fashions that reminded him of those cheesy sci-fi B-movies of his youth. Above him, frozen in the air, were machines that invoked cars but had no wheels and were mid-flight.

The future, he thought. It worked. This time everything didn't end.

He had just needed to remove himself from the equation and everything would work out OK for everyone. Humanity would still have a future, as long as he didn't contribute to it.

And with that, he was done. He knew deep inside, in some primal corner of his mind, that he accomplished what he had set out to do. Humanity would continue on now that he wasn't here to fuck it all up.

He wondered what was next. Would he feel anything? Would there be any sort of awareness after? After this incredible journey, would there be any more adventures?

With nothing else to do, Kevin reset reality with his mind and time resumed.

And then there was nothing at all—he was gone.

June 27, 1993
The Gas Station, Manhattan

GG Allin sat in the bathroom of the small, dank, dirty club.

The air was hot that night and the venue smelled like a mix of wet dog and gasoline. He was alone, but could hear the opening band through the rotten walls. His head swirled as the mish-mash of chemicals did their thing.

The no-name shitty band was just finishing their set and soon it would be time for him to go on. He'd been at a friend's house, which was practically next door, doing coke. He didn't want to deal with any of the opening bands or the poor, fucked-up souls who would bother to show up to something like this.

There was the instrument drone of the band finishing their last song and some half-hearted applause that quickly diminished to conversation.

He sat on the dirty toilet seat with his eyes closed. He had to psych himself up. He had to be ready to rage.

Bang—Bang—Bang

"Yo," said a voice from the other side of the bathroom door. "You ready? It's time."

"OK," said GG Allin.

He went out to perform and give it his all. He didn't know it would his last show.

Later that night, GG Allin would go to a party and die, drugged and depressed. His corpse would sit with no one knowing that he had passed on. Partygoers would pose with his body for pictures—thinking that he was just doing the junkie nod instead of a full respiratory failure. It would be several hours before anyone would think to check if he was OK.

GG Allin died and all was right with the world.

BATH SALT FETUS

Jorge Palacios

Being a pregnant teenager is hard; being a pregnant teenager in Puerto Rico can be downright infernal. This island is a shit-stain in the Caribbean, a hellhole seething with Catholic guilt, a judgmental attitude, and unfiltered sexism.

Maria was one of these teenagers. She came from a broken home, but found a family in the local punk scene. She explored every kind of experience she could find. She'd slept around since she was twelve. By fifteen, she was tattooed and pierced all over, and was sloppily learning to play bass so she could someday start her own punk band. For now though, she was forced to be part of normal society and was sent by her mother to the laundromat.

As she folded her laundry, she felt the eyes of other people in the establishment, staring at her huge belly, giving her looks, cursing at her in silence and laughing at her misfortune, a pure sense of satisfaction in them knowing they were superior to this underage hood rat.

Maria just wanted to throw the detergent at them with all kinds of swearing and hatred. She couldn't take it anymore, those stares judging every step she took, every breath released from her body. She wanted to return to normal. She wanted an abortion.

She begged her friends to loan her money for the abortion, but none of them wanted to give it, some out of catholic guilt, but most of them because they were broke, since they too lived with their parents, or on the streets. She even asked her mother. After her mother screamed at her and called her a murderer, the subject was put to rest.

As the clothing spun around and around, she wondered what she could do to get rid of this problem, this reminder of the loser she had let inside her body.

After a twenty-minute walk carrying a huge bag of warm, clean clothes, she made it to her low-income housing (which was also a notorious drug-selling area code-named Crackville).

"Mom?" she called. She waited for a response, but there was none, just the humming of the refrigerator. Maria walked in and looked around expecting to find her mother, who must have gone out. Good, Maria thought. The last thing she wanted was some speech about how the youth of today was going down the drain, save your soul before it's too late, blah, blah, blah. She dropped the laundry bag next to the refrigerator, grabbed an entire box of Oreos, and went to her room.

Her room was the only place she could get any kind of peace. The walls were decorated with posters from some of her favorite bands: Discharge, GBH, The Casualties, DRI, Gwar and The Mentors. Most of her wall space, however, was dedicated to her own personal Jesus, the only rock star she ever thought was genuine, the true King of Rock 'N' Roll (fuck Elvis!), Kevin Michael Allin, better known as GG. She had photos and posters from his young rock 'n' roller punk days to his last moments, when he looked like a beaten-up bulldog.

She turned on her stereo, blasting "Hated in the Nation" as she took her clothes off. Her pregnant body repulsed her. Stretch marks covered her huge belly. Her swollen nipples looked brown when they used to be pink. More upsetting was the fact that the nipple rings had to be taken out, and her stomach tattoos, which she loved to display, were stretched to the point of repugnance. She had tattooed the word "Mayhem" in bold, pointy black letters. Now it looked like it had been smeared on by a paintbrush.

She wanted to drown in the bottle of Jack Daniels she had been saving for the day she got rid of the fetus, the bottle that had been lying under the bed for three months now. As she grabbed it, her cell phone rang.

"Yes?" she answered.

"Hey bitch, it's me." Loca. The kind of friend you didn't like, but couldn't really get rid of either.

"Hey Loca, what's up?"

"You still trying to abort that baby?"

"Of course!" Maria shouted.

"Stay calm, I'm on my way."

Maria's mind raced as Loca hung up. What could she have meant? Did she have a way to get rid of the fetus? She paced the living room, eyes wide as a meth-head, throwing her phone from her right hand to her left.

The sun was going down by the time Loca reached Maria's apartment, and there was still no sign of Maria's mother. They greeted each other the way two old acquaintances would, shaking hands and awkwardly hugging, then sitting next to each other on the living room couch.

"What stinks, bitch?" Loca asked.

"What do you mean?"

"Don't you smell it?"

Maria shrugged.

"Well anyway," Loca continued after shrugging in unison, "I've got this great shit you have to try called Freezing Moon. It's a new kind of crystal meth, supposedly from Norway or some shit."

"Why should I try it?" Maria asked.

"Because, bitch, not only will it get you high as fuck, but you'll abort the baby naturally."

Maria never thought Loca's words could sound so beautiful, with her nasally tone and arrogant stance, but what she said was exactly what Maria wanted to hear.

Loca pulled out a bag of blue powder that looked like cleaning detergent. Maria felt disappointed. For some reason, she thought that this "natural abortion" drug would look more... epic.

"I hope this doesn't kill me," Maria said. She was only half-serious, as she was willing to die if it meant getting rid of this thing.

Loca said, "At least it's guaranteed not to give you an overdose."

After a half hour of gossip and drug talk, Loca left, leaving Maria alone with the blue powder. She stared at it, sitting on top of the living room table, almost as if it was staring back at her.

She really wanted a cigarette, but her mother had forced her to throw them out. Hey, where was her mother anyway? It was night and the crickets were in full swing. She shrugged it off. Her mother had probably found somebody from her church group to shack up with.

This was it, no more waiting around.

She rolled the Freezing Moon into a joint, lit it up, and took a deep suck. The power of this drug hit her almost immediately, and the usually warm Puertorrican weather turned ice cold. It ran down her veins and into her extremities, and up to her brain, like an electric shock. Her eyes became completely wide. She felt the sensation of riding a roller coaster, the ride moving faster and faster until her own skin started to peel, and her eyeballs detached from her skull. She screamed, and realized she was still in her apartment.

"This shit is awesome!"

She blasted one of her G.I.S.M. 7 inch records, and moshed around her living room, screaming loud Japanese nonsense that she thought was the lyrics. Once in a while she could feel the child inside her, kicking as if begging for her to stop, but she simply ignored it.

After fifteen minutes, the record ended and she blacked out on the couch. As she slept, she imagined herself falling from a mountain, hitting all the rocks on the way down and laughing the whole time.

She woke up two hours later, expecting to be on the side of a snowy precipice, but was instead lying on her couch. She looked around, trying to recollect what had happened, but the room looked spotless, and the only sound was the record skipping. She called for her mother again, but there was no answer. Where the hell was she? She was supposed to bring home a bucket of KFC.

"I'm starving!" Maria screamed. She rubbed her belly. She looked down at it and her frown grew deeper. "Fuck, I forgot I'm pregnant..."

She scratched her belly, and everything came back to her, especially Loca and her Freezing Moon drug bullshit. Sure, smoking it had made her feel awesome for a while, but it hadn't done what it was supposed to do. She was still preggo. She should have known Loca's tall tales were too good to be true. The lying bitch.

She began to scratch her belly deeper and deeper until she realized she had broken the skin. She looked at her fingers, covered in chunks of meat, and felt a weird energy inside her. She licked her fingers, and that energy went into her mouth as well. She had heard some weird stories about what meth could do to your body, especially from reality shows, and she wondered...

She got up from the couch and grabbed a knife from the kitchen. She cut into her arm, and the sensation that she felt ran all over her body. She let out a moan of pleasure as the blade sliced into her flesh and blood dripped onto the floor. That's when she realized the second side effect from this Freezing Moon meth strain: all the pain she should be feeling turned to sexual pleasure.

She let out a laugh, took off her clothes, and went to town on her body. She cut across her arms, her breasts, her thighs, her legs and her face, turning her once beautiful body into a road map of scarification and bleeding that turned the light blue carpeting into a dark mix of red and brown.

Then, as if in defiance of every "sanctity of life" speech she ever heard, she began to cut a target into her pregnant stomach.

She could not stop laughing. The orgasmic pain made her masturbate nonstop. She had multiple orgasms, the most intense coming when she slid the blade across her right nipple. It was the greatest moment of her life.

She sat on the floor, letting the energy flow and the blood

escape. She looked down on her belly. She knew now that her body would never abort her baby naturally with those drugs, but the pain just felt too good to stop.

She went to her room, leaving a trail of blood as she walked. She looked at the poster of a bloody GG Allin and smiled, knowing she looked so much like him that he would be proud. She grabbed a wire hanger from the closet, bent it enough so that it looked like a long hook, and grinned.

The bathroom was filthy and needed a good scrubbing, as there was a huge black mildew stain running from the showerhead to the drain, nasty and constantly wet. This was a bane to Maria's existence. She hated having to stand there and look at it as she cleaned herself. But today it didn't matter, as her blood was now darker than any bathtub shitstain could ever be.

Standing in the tub, she opened her legs, took a deep breath, and inserted the wire hanger into her vagina. As the metal hook entered, what should have been an incredible pain made her instantly wet. She prodded her insides with the hanger's tip and perforated her internal organs, achieving multiple orgasms and squirting twice before she finally hit something. It was hard and round, and it seemed to shift with her belly as she pulled on the wire. This had to be the baby. It wasn't fun pain, or orgasmic, or sexy. It was real.

As the thing inside her stretched her vagina and broke her privates apart, she moaned louder than any porn star. She orgasmed as she pulled out the head. The hanger's hook was buried deep inside the baby's eyeball. She counted one, two, three, and gave another big pull. Out slid the baby, blood, flesh, and umbilical cord all in one. It splashed into the bathtub with a loud thump. Maria screamed once again in pleasure, and her legs gave way. She collapsed.

For a couple minutes, she was in orgasmic ecstasy. She had never experienced anything like this with anyone, not with a man, or a woman, or a vibrator. Her heart pounded at a million beats per second, making her breathing quite painful. Her vision blurred, and she wasn't in control of her lips, drooling on herself like a panting dog.

"Hey, bitch!"

The voice was gruff and loud, like somebody with authority, or just a creep that had smoked way too many cigarettes. It called to her a couple times, but her ecstatic state prevented her from doing anything. After a few minutes, her eyesight returned to normal, and she could move just enough to look at the aborted fetus between her legs.

She expected it to be lying there, dead as fuck, purple and covered in flies. Instead, it was sitting down, umbilical cord wrapped around it's body like a fucked-up meat toga that lead to her vagina, clearly alive, and far more familiar than she could have imagined. It was shaped like a normal baby, with tiny but chubby features and a big clunky head, but it had fucked-up facial hair, was covered in bad tattoos, and it's penis was tinier than your typical baby dick. She recognized the creature immediately, but at the same time, she couldn't believe it.

"You're... you're..." Maria struggled to say it.

"Yeah, I'm GG Allin, bitch. Your drugs gave me the perfect opportunity to come back from the dead. Now I need you to cut that umbilical cord so I can be free."

The fetus pointed at the cord. Maria wanted to laugh out loud, more because of the absurdity of the situation than anything else. But she simply nodded. She grabbed the umbilical cord, and began to stretch it in an attempt to tear herself free of her child.

"No scissors, eh?" GG Allin said. "I guess you'll have to do it the old-fashioned way."

Maria laughed, lowered her head and bit into the cord. The meat and blood tasted foul, and she was disappointed that it didn't discharge the same level of orgasmic pain that her other mutilations had caused her. After a few big bites and some pulling, the chord detached.

GG Allin chuckled, and began to levitate, the umbilical cord wrapping around his tiny body.

"Thanks, you fucking slut!"

GG Allin grabbed the end of the cord, and inserted it into his anus. He pulled it in and out, in and out, and he moaned and groaned with pleasure.

"Oh yeah," GG said, "That's it. I love to fuck myself."

Maria laughed and nodded, remembering the song.

After a small ejaculation, which looked more like a mass of yellow pus and smelled like mayonnaise that had gone bad, GG removed the end of the cord from his anus, and wiped the shit that covered it all over his mouth. Maria just watched, fascinated. GG couldn't help but notice.

"What are you looking at?" GG screamed.

"I've always wanted to meet you," Maria said. "I'm your biggest fan. I've modeled my entire life on what you preach."

"Yeah?" the fetus replied. "Well, why don't you suck on my asshole?"

Maria thought about it, but GG interrupted her train of thought.

"Wait!" GG screamed. "Better yet, why don't we get some drugs?"

"It's really late."

"I don't give a fuck, you cocksucking cunt!" the fetus growled. "I need heroin!"

Maria stood still for a few seconds, staring at the stain that covered her tub, and thought about where she should take the fetus to get high. She then remembered that she was high, and looked at the fetus, smiling at his crooked, scarred face.

"I have a friend called Loca who has excellent drugs. We could go to her!"

"Lead the way, whore!"

Men, women, and children watched in horror as Maria walked down the street, completely nude and covered in blood and cuts, laughing maniacally, a blade still in her right hand. She did not know if people were looking at her or if they could see the creature following her.

GG Allin floated behind, sucking on his shit-covered

umbilical cord and singing some unintelligible song that sounded more like barking. For the ten minutes that it took her to walk to Loca's apartment, everybody stared, but nobody dared to say anything to her. She stepped on broken glass and other pieces of miscellaneous objects, and the pain gave her bliss.

She walked into Loca's building. An old Dominican lady saw her and ran away screaming, but Maria didn't even react. She got on the elevator and pressed the seventh floor button. She knocked on Loca's apartment door, quickly, anxiously.

Loca opened the door, her hair covered in rolls, and her face smeared in skin cream.

"What the fuck is wrong with you?" Loca screamed as she opened the door. Her attitude dropped immediately after she saw the state of Maria before her. "Oh my God!"

Maria pushed her way in. Loca fell back onto her apartment floor, too shocked to push back. Maria locked the door behind her, and raised her knife. She grinned, and Loca looked horrified at Maria's red eyes and teeth, stained from blood.

"What happened to you?"

"Never mind that," Maria yelled. "I need more drugs, like the one you gave me."

"Oh fuck, the Freezing Moon..." Loca said.

"Hurry up!" Maria screamed.

"I... I don't have anymore!"

Maria's smile turned into a frown, and slowly turned into anger.

"You lie!" Maria screamed.

Maria raised her knife, and ran toward Loca.

Loca raised her hands, trying to block the knife.

Loca's severed fingers splattered on the floor, her screaming continuing as Maria sliced and diced her body. Maria stabbed her repeatedly, until the forty-fourth stab, which went directly into the middle of Loca's chest. Loca collapsed completely, and pooped herself.

Maria struggled to take the knife out, but it seemed to be

stuck. After a couple of tries, she laughed again, drooling in her insanity.

"Mommy!"

Maria recognized the voice behind her, and turned around. GG Allin floated above her, poop falling from him onto the floor.

"Did you get the drugs, mommy?"

"No, darling," Maria said, "but I know exactly what you need."

Maria grabbed GG's umbilical cord, pulled the fetus to her.

She bit into him.

GG screamed and called her "cunt" and "bitch" repeatedly as Maria ripped off body part after body part. Blood and organs splashed on the floor and the walls of the apartment. The carnage went on until there was nothing of GG but a mess on the floor, and she digested it completely.

That's when the police kicked in Loca's apartment door. The sight of Maria, with Loca's dead body and tiny body parts that could only belong to a baby on the floor, turned their faces pale white and made them raise their weapons, ordering her to lie down.

As they entered, Maria again tried to pull the knife out of Loca's chest, succeeding and swinging it at the officers.

When they shot off her hand, she felt the bullet penetrate, and saw, as if in slow motion, the meat and the fingers explode, splashing into the air and to her face. The feeling of warm meat and plasma was electric. It went the same way as the panic-stricken officers let out bullet after bullet, breaking into her body with splashes of gore flying across the floor. Each one was like a jolt on her vagina, a never-ending vibrator, her body a huge clitoris, charged completely.

Was this death? Wasn't it supposed to be more morbid? She laughed out loud, and had an intense orgasm.

DREAM QUEST FOR DOPE

John Bruni

"Dude! Why didn't you kill yourself tonight? I paid, like, ten bucks for this ticket. What the fuck?"

GG Allin didn't even break stride. Barely aware of the beer bottle in his hand, he smashed it upside the guy's head. Long hair flung up in a sweaty tangle, and the guy fell on his back, rolling like a turtle. Not that GG noticed. He strode with purpose away from the ugly scene, rage boiling in his head. The cocksuckers hadn't even let him finish his show. Fuckers.

The guy, still on the ground, started giggling. "Dude! GG Allin just broke a fucking bottle over my head! That rules!"

Dressed only in a skirt and combat boots, body soiled with his own feces, GG somehow managed to hail another cab, and this time, the driver didn't freak out. GG slumped into the backseat and closed his eyes, trying to banish the clusterfuck of a show from his mind. He thought about the dope the promoter had scored for him. Ten lovely bags. That should be enough to do the trick.

When he got back to St. Mark's, he went up to his room and went for his works. Cooked. Shot. And let chemical bliss take him down from a day's worth of deli coke and booze. The comforting cloud filled his head and lungs like cotton candy, and it felt so wonderful he had to remind himself to breathe. He rested with a soiled arm over his equally soiled face and rode the wave of dopamine.

But it wore off too fast. Cheap shit. Did GG really expect something more from the asshole at the Gas Station? You couldn't trust people anymore, could you?

He could only trust in one thing, and he stumbled around the room, seeking out his private stash. There, taped under the bottom of one of the dresser's drawers, he found a rolled up baggie. Unfortunately, the contents left much to be desired. There was so little, he might as well not even bother.

But . . . well, maybe on top of the cheap shit, it would do the job. It might be just enough to get him into that headspace to get more.

Just as he prepared to cook again, Johnny Puke and the girls showed up. From there, it was a whirlwind of shit. Just a few more bumps and some whiskey to even it all out, and the next thing GG knew, they were at Johnny's place, snorting more cheap-shit dope. GG hated putting heroin up his nose, but Johnny hated needles.

Distantly, he hoped he'd packed up his works before leaving St. Mark's. He checked the pockets of his jean jacket. Thank fuck. It was there. He barely heard himself telling the others he had to take a shit, and soon, he perched on the toilet in the bathroom, preparing the last batch. It took him a moment to find a good vein. So many had collapsed of late, he started looking at the ones in his feet. Not yet, though. This shot deserved a special place.

A spaghetti noodle of a blue vein rose ever so slightly from the back of his hand, and he made quick work of it. As he depressed the plunger, he whispered the words he'd learned so long ago, words that would make no sense to anyone else save for the select few who pursued forbidden knowledge. Not even he knew what they meant, but he knew that they would get him the most potent dope he'd ever had and lots of it.

This shit got him in a place the garbage Johnny gave him couldn't reach. It went deep, scratching an itch deep in his bones. The world became hazy, and he stashed his works, knowing it would be his last chance to do so before the super dope hit him full force.

In a haze, he staggered out of the bathroom and donned his ragged jean jacket. Johnny jabbered about some kind of European tour, but with no music. Just words. Fuck that. GG wanted to scare the shit out of people, and a lecture just wouldn't cut it.

46

Numbness burned slightly throughout his limbs, and he thought he'd close his eyes for a minute. He got down on the floor and stared at the ceiling, waiting for the rush, the rush that no other dope had ever offered him.

His eyelids fell, and while his companions thought he had just passed out, GG found himself hurtling through the cosmos. He didn't know how many stars he'd passed, and he never questioned why he didn't need an astronaut suit while in space, but before long he flew through mist and into the Dreamlands.

When he opened his eyes, he didn't see the desert. Nor did he see the mountains and the sun. Instead, he found himself in a dank cemetery full of broken stones and rotting trees. Tombs yawned open and hoary graves all sported deep holes, their contents long since raided.

"What the fuck?" GG said. "This ain't Leng."

"You're off by several thousand miles."

GG whirled on the strange voice and found himself confronted with a grungy, dog-faced man with long, yellowed fingernails and jagged teeth. The man stank of the grave, and when he breathed, the odor of rotten meat wafted over. GG barely noticed through the screen of his own filthy stink, and that alone impressed him.

"Who the fuck are you?" he asked.

"In days of old, I was a painter by the name of Pickman," the creature said. "Now I'm but a lowly ghoul. The worm flails, you know."

GG didn't know, and he didn't care. "Painter? What kind of shit did you do?"

"Ghastly stuff, old boy. Things that turned the stomachs of the high and mighty."

"I can dig that. I do some pretty fucked up art. You should see 'Blood, Shit & Cum.'"

Pickman sneered. "Sounds . . . wonderful."

GG grabbed the ghoul's ratty shirt and yanked him close. Then, without ceremony, he head-butted Pickman, opening a gash up on the painter's forehead.

Pickman yelped and staggered back, holding his face. "Why?"

"You talk shit, you get hit. Now tell me how to get to Leng."

Pickman's lower lip quivered. "No. You struck me. You can find help elsewhere."

GG stepped forward, reaching out, and Pickman backed away, lightning fast. Pickman jumped on top of a gravestone. Perched like a raven, he didn't even sway. This didn't deter GG, who rushed the ghoul, face screwed up in a snarl. Again, Pickman leaped away, this time into the cradle of a creaky tree bough above.

"Stop," he said. "You can't catch me."

GG kicked the tree, his combat boots hitting solidly. The tree gave out a shriek, and the deadwood snapped in two, sending Pickman sprawled out on the loam. Before the ghoul could scrabble to his feet, GG grabbed a handful of his hair and yanked his head back.

"No! Stop! I'll help you! Just don't hit me!"

GG released Pickman's hair but gave him a solid kick to the ass, sending the ghoul rolling away. Moaning, Pickman managed to stand up, rubbing at his backside. "Why do you want to go to Leng? There is nothing for mortals there."

"My dealer lives there," GG said. "He's got the best shit I've ever had, and I need my fix."

"Ah." Understanding washed over Pickman's face, and he smiled. "*That* I can understand. It's very powerful and dangerous, but it is also very good. You are a long way from Leng. It would take you weeks, and while you're in the Dreamlands, it would still be too arduous a journey. There are so many things that can go wrong. Gods, monsters, death in all shapes and sizes."

"I don't give a fuck."

"By the time you got there, you wouldn't need Leng's opiates. You will have kicked the habit."

"Then think of a way to get me there quicker." GG's hands balled up into fists without him realizing it.

Pickman noticed right away. Message received. "I could help you, but I would want something in return. I've been seeking out a friend, Randolph Carter, from days gone by. The last I heard, he was in an alien's body. I would like—"

"No." GG didn't need to say another word.

"But . . ." Pickman saw the resolve in GG's face and knew he wouldn't be able to barter with this man. The need for Leng's pleasures was too strong in his soul. "Fine. You'll need a Nightgaunt. That will make the journey much shorter. You'd be in Leng within the hour."

"Good. Go get me one."

It had been a while since Pickman had summoned and bound a creature, and he didn't know if he could do it. Still, he understood the Dreamlands very well, and he knew he had a lot of power here. He had to try it. Besides, he wanted to get rid of GG. The sooner this lunatic was gone, the sooner Pickman could get back to his life of seclusion.

GG sat on a grave and watched Pickman go to work. He created a circle of stones and lit some candles. He said some mumbo jumbo bullshit, like the kind that brought GG here in the first place. He still couldn't figure out how that had gone wrong. It never had before. How fucked up had he been when he tried?

Not fucked up enough. He got bored and started throwing rocks at tree trunks. More often than not, his arm was strong enough to knock the fuckers over. It gave him an idea for a song, but he didn't have anything to write on. He thought about writing in his own shit on a gravestone and tried to squeeze out a couple of turds. Unfortunately, the opiates in his system had blocked him up. All he managed was a timorous fart.

The sky darkened, and GG looked up to see a gangly monster with giant talons and wings gliding down from the heavens. It looked cool as all shit. The fact that it didn't have a face thrilled him even more. He wondered what those assholes back in the real world would think if he confronted them with one of these. He wished he could bring it back with him.

The Nightgaunt softly landed in front of Pickman and knelt before him, offering its back. Pickman spoke to it, pointing at GG. It turned its faceless head toward GG and waited.

"It's all yours," Pickman said. "It knows exactly where to bring you. Just climb on its back, and you're ready to go."

GG hopped up on the creature's back, gripping its leathery flesh with his balled up fists. He could probably stab this fucker and the blade would break.

"Good luck," Pickman said.

"Hold it," GG said. "Where do you think you're going?"

"I summoned the Nightgaunt for you. My job here is done."

"Climb up behind me. You're coming with me."

Pickman grimaced. "Why?"

"Because you're a useful fucker. I want you with me if I need something."

Pickman sighed, resigned to his fate. Just to avoid another altercation—his head still stung from being butted earlier—he climbed up on the Nightgaunt and held on tight to GG's waist.

"Get your hands off me," GG said.

He did not have to ask twice. Pickman clutched at the Nightgaunt's back, tightening his legs around it, hoping that would be enough.

"How do you get this thing to go?"

Pickman uttered one word in ancient Plutonian, hoping that the velocity of take-off would be enough to send GG off into the ether, never to return. The Nightgaunt soared into the sky at a frightening speed, but GG held on so tightly the beast's back creaked.

Cold wind cut through to GG's bones, and tears welled up in his eyes. He kept blinking, trying to keep them warm, but it only produced more moisture, forcing it out into streams that cut through the shit still smeared on his face. His teeth ground together as he bunched his muscles up to tighten his grip. Behind him, Pickman whined. It was hard to hear with the rush of air all around them, but it disgusted GG. He wondered how Pickman would cope with one of his concerts. Pussy.

Land flashed below them, changing from dank forest to farmland to village and back again. GG marveled at how fast the Nightgaunt could go. Fuck cars and trains and shit. If he could travel by Nightgaunt in the real world, he'd do it every time. He lifted a fist defiantly into the air and loosed a primal howl, most of it lost to the wind. *This* was rock and roll. Perfect for the one true king.

Woods gave way to mountains, and they soon gave way to desert. Almost there. They soared over the endless sand, dotted with the occasional sun-bleached skeleton. When he saw the plains ahead, he knew he'd reached Leng in record time. It had felt only like a half an hour. Not bad.

The Nightgaunt descended until it skimmed over the surface of the world. Domiciles were holes in the ground, and they were everywhere. People loitered and roamed, going about their daily business, but they weren't really people. Those in Leng looked like the satyrs of ancient Greece: naked to the waist and covered with fur from there on down. Hooves instead of feet. Horns crowning their heads. Giant cocks swaying between their legs. And the most frightening grins known to humanity, full of a carnivore's sharp, pointy teeth.

GG recognized this village, and he steered the Nightgaunt until they reached his dealer's place, at which point the beast slowed to a hover and flapped its way to the ground.

Pickman fell off, his hands bunched into tight fists. Grimacing, he tried to open his fingers, but they were too stiff, and his muscles ached from holding onto the Nightgaunt so tightly. He didn't think he could stand.

GG stepped down with a bit more dignity. He flexed his hands to get some of the creakiness out of them and glanced at Pickman's pathetic form. GG shook his head and approached his dealer's home. He positioned himself over the hole and put both hands around his mouth in a funnel shape. "Yo! You home?"

"I'm coming!"

GG stepped back and waited, listening to the scrabbling sound of someone ascending the ladder. Soon, a Leng man poked his horned head out of the hole and smiled. "GG! I've been expecting you."

"Then you know what I need, Yith Wagge," GG said.

"You liked the batch I gave you?"

"Fucking loved it. I need more. How much?"

Yith climbed the rest of the way out, showing himself to be shorter than average. He squinted up into GG's eyes with an odd expression. GG thought it might be regret. That son of a bitch better not hold out on him. GG was in a head-butting mood.

"About that," Yith said.

"You better have my shit."

Yith's grin turned into a pained smile. "You know how I've been expecting you?" He didn't wait for GG to respond. "It's because you've, um, been summoned here."

"What the fuck does that mean?"

Pickman felt an odd sensation in his stomach, kind of like whenever he thought about Carter's dream quest so long ago. While GG was distracted, Pickman inched toward the Night-gaunt.

"It means that someone wanted you here," Yith said. "We have a visitor, and he'd like to talk with you."

A gust of wind blew out of the hole, and a figure levitated stiffly out, setting himself down gently next to GG. The stranger had dark skin, and he wore robes and gold as a pharaoh of Egypt would, topped off with a regal turban. A long goatee grew from his chin like a handle, and his dark eyes gazed majestically out from thick eyeliner.

"Who the fuck is this?" GG asked. "You a cop?"

"You're late," the stranger said, "but that's fine. I caused your trajectory to vary slightly, just to give us enough time."

GG turned back to Yith. "What the fuck's going on? Where's my dope?"

Yith shrugged. "It's not my show. Sorry, man. I really am."

GG turned back to the stranger, about a hair's length away from trashing him from foot to turban. Yet when he looked into the stranger's eyes, he felt odd. Not necessarily high, but distant. The rushing blood in his veins slowed, and he felt himself falling under the stranger's sway.

"We've been waiting for a remarkable man like you for centuries," the stranger said. "Your dedication to danger is second to none. You live your life without lies, suffering no one. There haven't been many like you throughout history. I'd wager you're one of a kind."

"You gonna suck my dick now?" GG asked. His words slurred, as if some force wanted him sedated, but nothing could stop these words from escaping him.

"You are seen by your fellow man as utterly disgusting," the stranger continued. "A pariah on nearly all fronts, except for your loyal followers, the ones who love it when you strike them and fling feces at them. In short, you're a disgrace to society, which makes you the perfect gate."

"For what?" GG asked. This surprised him. He didn't give a fuck, but something inside him wanted to find out more about the stranger's plans for him. He tried to draw back his fist for a punch, but his arm remained limp at his side.

The stranger produced a crystal ball from his robe and held it aloft. "Look, GG Allin. Back to the waking world."

An image materialized in the crystal, and it was Johnny and the girls. And there was GG himself on the floor in the background, passed out. A Polaroid camera came out, and Johnny posed with GG, grinning drunkenly.

"Your friends don't know it yet," the stranger said, "but you're dying. Soon, they will retire for the evening, and when they wake, they'll find your corpse."

"I'm not dying," GG said. "I'm right here."

"Your dream self is right here, but I assure you, your physical body is dying. Too much heroin, as I'm sure you can surmise. Right now, you're suffering from respiratory failure.

53

Right away, GG knew the stranger was telling the truth. It made sense after a life of insanity, and he didn't even feel bad about it. He only regretted not being able to kill himself on stage. That would have been awesome.

"You're not in your body," the stranger said. "When you die, you'll be stuck here. Your reanimated corpse will be our gateway to the waking world. My kind will pour through and completely destroy humanity. They don't deserve their planet, anyway. We're clearing the way for a new race."

"You mean, I'm going to cause the end of the world?"

"The end of the human race," the stranger said.

GG smiled. That was even better than onstage suicide. "Cool."

The stranger glanced sidelong at him. "This doesn't bother you?"

"No." GG shook his head faintly, almost sadly. "Those assholes have become complacent. In the tooth and claw world, they wouldn't survive. It's time to remind them of that, don't you think?"

This time, the stranger laughed so hard he almost dropped his crystal ball. Out of breath, he put it back into his robe. "You truly are a remarkable man, GG Allin."

"Nah. Hank Williams, that dude was remarkable."

"I'm familiar with him. He made the journey to the Dreamlands, as well. I'm sure if you wander long enough you'll find him. Do you want to watch the end of your kind?"

"I don't give a fuck. I just want my dope."

Yith cleared his throat and kneaded his hands together. "There's, um, no dope. That other batch was made specifically to lure you here. It would take years to make more."

GG stared at him. "There's. No. Dope."

Yith grinned sheepishly, producing a tiny baggie with some of the super dope in it. "This is all I have left. It's not even worth using. Might as well just get some black tar."

The stranger said, "We can always get you something else. We have dreamers bringing new drugs in every day. It's only a matter of time bef—"

54

GG shot forward like a dart and brought his forehead down on the bridge of the stranger's nose. A sharp crack resonated down the plain, and the stranger gargled as blood filled his throat. His nose looked cracked in half, and the bottom of his face shone red in the sun.

"You dare?!" the stranger said through crimson slobber. "You dare head-butt Nyarlathotep, messenger of the Outer Gods?!"

GG kicked Nyarlathotep's kneecap, snapping it backward. The Outer God fell to his hind, snarling. Then, just as GG stepped forward to deal another blow, Nyarlathotep's face split down the center, and a gigantic tentacle emerged. His shape grew, and his skin split. His shoes exploded, revealing not feet, but hooves.

Pickman almost made it. When GG started beating the stranger, Pickman had managed to reach the Nightgaunt and was about to jump on its back and make his escape. Then, he saw Nyarlathotep bursting through the skin of the man, showing off one of his other forms.

Panic rushed through Pickman's body, and he felt like he'd been touched by lightning. He wanted nothing more than to get away from this horrible mess. But he couldn't let Nyarlathotep be loosed in Leng. Somehow, Nyarlathotep had to be dismissed.

Once upon a time, Randolph Carter had given Pickman a stone with an odd design on it. He'd told Pickman that it would ward off even the toughest of gods, should he ever need it. Now, he fished through his ratty pockets, seeking it out. He weeded through a few spare bones and some lint before he finally found it at the very bottom.

GG watched as Nyarlathotep shed the final vestige of his human form. It didn't have much effect on him, though. He'd seen a lot of crazy shit in the Dreamlands, and this was just one more thing. He wondered if he could jump up high enough to head-butt Nyarlathotep now.

In that moment, Pickman lunged between the two of them, holding aloft the elder sign. "Back, Nyarlathotep! Get you gone!"

Nyarlathotep shrank back from Pickman like a vampire from a cross. Then Pickman started babbling in another language. GG thought it sounded like nonsense, but it had too much cadence to be anything but actual speech.

Nyarlathotep turned his red, blazing three-lobed eyes to GG. "It's too late. As soon as you die, the human race will end, and we'll have our way with your miserable planet."

GG didn't care about humanity. How could anyone take the fat bodies seriously? He did care that this piece of shit, who didn't even have the super dope from Leng, was going to get his way. Fuck that. He stepped toward the Nightgaunt, but he then saw Yith, cowering away from them. He still clutched the baggie.

Yith noticed GG staring at him and gauged the distance between himself and the hole in the ground where he lived. It did not look good to him.

He didn't have to think about it much longer. GG threw a haymaker into Yith's jaw, knocking the Leng man into unconsciousness long before his head hit the ground. GG swiped the baggie and jammed it into his pocket. Only then did he turn back to the Nightgaunt. He stepped around Pickman.

"What are you doing?" the ghoul asked.

GG ignored him as he got on the beast's back and thought about how Pickman had gotten this thing going before. He thought he remembered, but he would probably butcher it. He sighed and leaned toward its ear. Gently, he whispered the Plutonian word, and the Nightgaunt took off immediately.

Land shrank away as they soared into the sky. Clouds swirled as if they were going down a drain, and GG felt his stomach drop down to his feet. They flew higher and higher, and he could hear his ears popping. He hazarded a look down and saw that even Nyarlathotep from this height seemed like a doll on a play set.

Then, GG let go of the Nightgaunt and felt himself fall away from the beast. He dropped like a stone, but he didn't like that he was falling backwards. He managed to turn himself around so he could watch the ground rush up at him. He never understood those pussies who wanted to be knocked out for surgery. He always wanted to be awake so he could watch what the doctors were doing to him.

The figures below became larger and larger as he came closer and closer to the ground. Nyarlathotep tried to get around Pickman and his elder sign, but the ghoul remained steadfast, keeping the Outer God at bay.

"No!" Nyarlathotep roared.

GG grinned, and his lips flapped about his face in the wind. Then, just before he struck the ground, he gave the god the middle finger.

He hit the sand so hard he could see every grain of it in stark clarity, and then he passed through it into the cosmos. Stars and planets whirled around him as he blasted through galaxies like a rocket. He pinwheeled through existence, leaving a vapor trail behind him as he came closer to the Milky Way. Closer to the Oort Cloud. Through the Kuiper Belt and past the gas giants. Plowing through the asteroid belt and Mars. And there!

Earth.

His trajectory slowed until he floated through the atmosphere. Through the roof of Johnny's apartment. Into the living room. Hovering above his physical body. He eased into the cradle of his flesh, and he felt almost grateful to be home, even though he could sense his impending death.

GG struggled for consciousness, desperate to see if he'd managed to bring the super dope back with him, but his body was too far gone. Fuck.

Too bad the human race didn't die, though. That would have been a hell of a thing to have to explain at the pearly gates. Not that GG believed any of that shit, not after everything his father had put him through. But still.

It could have been a kick ass song.

The next day, after they'd found GG's body, his friends tried to hide all their drugs before calling the cops. Johnny Puke patted down GG's jacket, just to make sure, and he found a small bag. There was hardly anything in it, but it looked different. Sparkly. Potent, almost like magic.

He stashed it away. For later. He couldn't wait to try out the shit that killed GG Allin.

THERE'S A LITTLE GG IN ALL OF US

Kevin Strange

Doctor Wendel opened the door to the waiting room and found GG Allin bent over the examination table with three of his own fingers stuck up his ass.

"Um. Mr..." Dr. Wendel checked his clipboard notes. "Allin. How can I, uh... help you today?"

GG stood up, leaving his filthy pants on the floor. He smelled his fingers. "Can't shit, motherfucker!"

Dr. Wendel wasn't sure if his patient was calling him a motherfucker or just cursing at the magnitude of his situation. "I see. Well, I'd like to go ahead and get a routine checkup out of the way. I don't seem to have any medical history for you..."

"Never been to no doctor. Don't need no fuckin' doctor. Don't give a fuck about no checkup."

"I see," Dr. Wendel said, scratching his thick black mustache. "Well, you did come to my office, so..."

"Told ya! Can't shit! How the fuck am I supposed to fucking do my shows if I can't fucking shit, MOTHERFUCKER!"

Dr. Wendel was fairly sure that "motherfucker" was directed at him. In his old college days, he'd karate chop this asshole right in the gizzard and be done with him. Dr. Wendel was six-foot-four and a very burly black man. Not many people would get up from his karate chops. Not without medical assistance, anyway. But it wasn't his college days, and he'd grown up a lot since then. It would take more than some punk rock weirdo to get him to lose his cool.

Besides, this GG Allin creep looked like he was routinely karate chopped in the gizzard. He was an ugly, bald fellow with wiry facial hair that reminded Dr. Wendel of a goat. His head was all scared up like it had been split open on many occasions by fists, bottles, and god knows what else. He doubted the dirty little punk would learn anything from a karate chop experience. Or worse, the punk might get off on it.

"Ok, Mr. Allin. It says here you're having trouble defecating. Bend over and we'll see if we can get to the bottom of this. Heh. Get it? No? Never mind. Doctor-patient humor."

After some more cursing and a few failed attempts at punching the doctor, GG finally bent over the table and relaxed, allowing Dr. Wendel to examine his asshole.

Treating his patient's anus like contaminated nuclear fallout, the doctor put on his elbow length gloves and face mask with shield. He wasn't about to take any chances. This guy seemed like the type that would set a doctor's appointment strictly for the purpose of shitting directly into his face.

Pushing past the crusted dingle berries, Dr. Wendel inserted his fingers into GG's anus and conducted his examination. Afterward, the doctor stood and crossed his arms.

"Well, I didn't find anything conclusive up there, Mr. Allin."

"Why the fuck can't I shit?!"

"I'm not sure. Have you changed your diet recently? Eating anything new that might have you constipated? You may be backed up further inside your bowel than I can see with an exterior examination. I could set up an endoscopic—"

"I eat shit and whiskey and whatever the fuck I want. What the fuck is it to you, motherfucker? You want me to eat your shit? I fucking will, asshole! Fucking motherfucker! FUCK YOU!"

Dr. Wendel was growing uncomfortable. He felt that old college tingle at the back of his neck. Was he really going to have to beat up this dirty creep right here in his own office?

"I said fuck you, motherfucker!" GG jumped off the table. Even though he was a head and a half shorter than the doctor, he stood toe to toe with the bigger man, dead set on starting a fight right there in the examination room.

No. Dr. Wendel wasn't going to fight him. Not at work,

anyway. He'd gladly show the little bastard what a fifth degree black belt in Taekwondo could do to his ugly face if they were at a bar, but this GG Allin character wasn't worth his general practitioner's license. No, the doctor had a better idea.

"I'll fucking fuck your fucking face, mother—"

The doctor thumped the little man on the forehead, freezing him in his tracks, mid-profanity. If he was going to talk reason to this weirdo, he was going to have to do it face to face.

"Ok, come out of there. Let's talk!"

Kneeling down so he could look GG Allin in the eyes, the doctor thumped the same spot on his own forehead and froze in place.

A piston sounded in GG's head and the top half of his dirty face lifted up and back like a trashcan lid, leaving his throat, tongue and the bottom half of his mouth exposed. The same happened to the doctor's head.

After the plague of 2743 took nearly 5 billion lives, all humans began living in colonies inside giant robot representations of people in order to avoid the contaminated air, and also as a convenient way to fight the genetically modified animals that reacted to the plague by growing upwards of a thousand times their original size. Now even the most cuddly albino shrew was the size of a dragon compared a human.

After several seconds of awkward silence, a tiny replica of the doctor wiggled up out of the esophagus of the larger body and walked out to the edge of the tongue. The smaller version of the doctor shouted, "Come out! Come talk to me!"

Even though the plague had been eradicated, people still stayed inside their robots, for the most part. But opening their heads to speak to one another in the flesh was not unheard of. There was little danger from mutant animal attacks inside the doctor's office, after all.

GG's throat started to wiggle and gyrate. Eventually, several dozen naked, screaming miniature versions of the punk rocker climbed out of the hole and ran full speed to the end of big GG's tongue. All of them were covered in filth, carrying huge balls of fecal matter. The ones at the front of the pack threw their balls of shit before being knocked off the tongue by the ones behind, cursing and yelling, pointing middle fingers in the air as they fell to their demise, splattering against the tile floor below.

Mini Doctor Wendel ducked behind some molars, doing his best to avoid the shit storm hurled in his direction. So that was the problem. With most of the population decimated by the plague that exploded people's entrails out their ears, eyes, noses and mouths before said entrails grew mouths of their own and consumed the entire host bodies, the new global government had used the tremendous wealth of the world to install cloning machines inside the bodies of the giant robots in order to speed up repopulation. What good was a planet, after all, with no consumers from which to generate profit? It looked as if the clone machine inside the GG Allin robot had malfunctioned. Dr. Wendel wondered what demented government official was evil enough to green light turning this god awful GG Allin into a robot in the first place.

Little GGs continued to pour out of the robot's throat. They now crowded around the entire mouth area, fighting each other, starting circular mosh pits, and in a few instances, performing oral and anal sex on one another.

Within minutes, coolers full of cheap beer were passed up through the giant throat, and all the GGs got incredibly drunk. It was pandemonium. No wonder the robot couldn't shit. His entire body was crammed with mini versions of himself. Which begged the question, how in the world was there still cold beer down there?

Dr. Wendel shuddered at the thought of the kind of vile, repugnant things that must go on inside a fifty-story robot populated entirely by miniature versions of someone like GG Allin. He didn't have much time to think about that awful fantasy before the reality hit him square in the face, literally.

A poop bomb exploded on his head, dripping down

into his eyes. Instinctively, he jumped up, retching, and tried to brush the fecal bomb off his head, only to be assaulted by dozens more. It was like a snowball fight with a side of E Coli.

Dr. Wendel had no choice but to retreat back down his robot's esophagus to the hatch that led into the robot proper. While cleaning up and changing clothes, an idea came to him.

"Brilliant!" he exclaimed as he pulled on a new white lab coat. Jogging down to the clone lab, he searched through the files and found exactly what he was looking for.

Minutes later he opened the hatch and ascended to the surface world once again, but this time, not alone. The GG Allin that lived inside Dr. Wendel's Dr. Wendel robot looked at Dr. Wendel confused. "What the fuck is going on up here? You promised me booze, shithead!"

"You have to calm those freaks down before they..."

Dr. Wendel ducked a poop grenade and crouched behind the robot's teeth again.

GG stood tall, scratching his balls. "Before what? Looks like they're partying it up over there. HEY!"

Dr. Wendel yanked at GG's pant leg. "No! Don't get their attention yet!"

"TOSS ME A FUCKIN' BEER, YOU FUCKS!"

Several cans hurled across the chasm between the robots and smacked the new GG directly in the head, instantly drawing blood, knocking him out cold.

Frustrated, Dr. Wendel jumped up and addressed the crowd of GGs. "Please! Listen to me! You all need to go back inside the robot and someone needs to switch off the cloning machine! Your robot's waste elimination orifice is clogged with what I presume to be more versions of you! It will overheat and explode if the orifice is not cleared soon! Please! You're all in danger!"

While the doctor was speaking, several naked GG Allins lined up at the teeth line of their robot, getting as close to the doctor bot as possible. They each grabbed their penises and worked up erections, laughing and screaming what may have been song lyrics. Then another GG shattered a beer bottle on an incisor and proceeded to run down the line, castrating each of the jerking GGs. The maimed GGs leaned back and pointed their nubby stumps in the air, showering the doctor in dick blood.

Wiping the fluid from his eyes, the doctor ran up to the teeth line of his own robot. "WHAT THE FUCK IS WRONG WITH YOU PEOPLE? DON'T YOU GIVE A SINGLE FUCK ABOUT YOUR OWN LIVES?"

The mosh pit stopped. The singing fell silent. All the GGs in the mouth of the GG robot stood still, watching the doctor.

"Well... that's better," the doctor said, composing himself. "Now, I need some volunteers to descend into the bowels of your robot so that you can..."

The GG from the doctor's robot had regained consciousness, slammed his beers, and crept up behind the doctor. The other punk rocker clones hadn't stopped what they were doing to listen to the doctor's plan to save their robot. They'd stopped to see if this other GG would be able to sneak up to the doctor and shove him off the robot's mouth before he noticed.

As Dr. Wendel plummeted to his death, the party resumed and the GGs rejoiced. Several of the castrated GGs even jumped after him just to heckle, spit at, piss on out of their nubs, or otherwise humiliate the doctor as he fell the fifty stories to the office floor.

"You fucks better get over here!" the lone GG on the giant doctor's tongue shouted. "The inside of this robot is fucking boring as fucking shit!"

The party GGs grabbed a naked, shit covered clone and swung him back and forth from his arms and legs, gaining momentum until they let go at the peak of their swing, only to miss the other robot's mouth by several feet, sending yet another GG Allin clone to his demise below.

The clone in Dr. Wendel's robot cackled while smashing his last empty beer can on his own head, creating a gash that soon bloodied his entire face. "Use your goddamn heads, you dumb shits!"

Several GG clones knelt down at the teeth line of their robot and held on to another clone's legs as he hung off the side. Another clone climbed down the first and grabbed onto the first clone's ankles.

"Fuck! They're building a bridge from their own bodies! We have to do something now!"

A small crowd of citizens had gathered at the throat hatch of the Dr. Wendel robot. A frumpy, balding man who looked as though he hadn't seen the sun in many years led the group. He carried a laser rifle he'd grabbed from the artillery room as they made their way up to the mouth of the robot, and now he stuck it out of the hatch and aimed it at the bloody faced GG.

"Wait, Marshall. We don't know if they'll even make it over here," a fit, middle-aged woman with a high, youthful voice said. She carried a pair of twin laser swords. "If we draw their attention now, they'll never stop 'til they take our robot too. You know how crazy just one of those guys is!"

Indeed, Marshall knew just how dangerous their GG Allin was. He'd been quarantined inside the Dr. Wendel robot for starting riots with his punk music before Dr. Wendel had used his security clearance to bring him to the surface. It had been a desperate move that Marshall had disagreed with from the start. But since it was Dr. Wendel's robot, Dr. Wendel had the final say.

And now Dr. Wendel was dead. Marshall was in charge now. And he had no intention of letting those degenerate punk rockers take over his robot on his watch.

"I don't want to hear that pussy shit from you right now, Rhonda. It's us or them!" Marshall charged out of the hatch and blasted bloody faced GG in the back with laser fire, ripping his torso clean in half. He haphazardly fired at the group standing in the other robot's mouth, slicing through heads, arms, legs and free swinging dicks with reckless abandon until the battery on the laser rifle blinked red, indicating it needed several minutes to recharge before it was ready to fire again.

Rhonda cursed under her breath and ran out after Marshall. The small group of citizens stepped out of the hatch behind her, carrying various laser weapons.

The clone bridge was already swinging its way over to the Dr. Wendel robot mouth by the time she caught up to her careless leader.

Marshall ran up to the teeth line and pointed at the swinging clones. "Chop their fucking arms off when they swing over he—GAHHH!!!"

The top half of bloody faced GG bit Marshall on the ankle, causing the headstrong leader to fall over backwards, dragging bloody face's dying torso over the ledge. Falling to the floor below, the flailing bodies resembled a kite as the innards of the dismembered GG flapped and fluttered in the air like a tail.

"Fuck this!" Rhonda screamed as she dodged shit, beer bottles, cum, piss and everything else the GG Allin horde threw at her from across the chasm.

The horde waiting to cross the clone bridge picked up the dismembered parts of their fallen brethren and swung arms and legs like clubs, ready to beat the citizens of Dr. Wendel's robot to death.

She even caught a glimpse of one of the clones face-fucking the decapitated head of his unlucky double.

"Retreat! Close the fucking mouth! Do you hear me in there! Shut the fucking mouth and lock the goddamn hatch before they get across!"

💀💀💀

"Hey, uh... Doc?" the next patient said as he entered the office. "There's a bald guy with half a mustache out in your waiting room with no clothes on, um.... pooping in your potted plants."

Dr. Wendel looked up from his clipboard. "Hm? Yeah, yeah. We fixed him right up, didn't we? Came in here with some constipation. Guess he was too excited to wait 'til he got home!" The doctor laughed, a little too loud and long for his patient's comfort.

"Oh. Ok. Well, um. I've been having pains in my arm lately and I'm concerned it might have something to do with my heart. Jesus doc! What happened in here? Is that blood all over the floor?"

"Yes," Dr. Wendel said, smiling wide. "The nurse told me about your arm. We'll get you fixed right up. Why don't you come lie down over here on the table so I can shit in your fucking mouth and watch you swallow it, you fat cunt fucker?"

"WHAT?" The patient backed away, eyeballing the door.

"Oh, don't be like that Mr. Smith! I'm kidding. Doctor-patient humor?"

"O-ok," Mr. Smith said, reluctantly stepping further into the office.

"Really, though. Get on the table and lie down."

ANARCHY CAFE

Nick Cato

New Hampshire, early 1985

It started as soon as he left her apartment.

If he hadn't known better, GG would have sworn a hamster was running amuck in his penis. He pushed down on the bulge in his pants, but the uncomfortable sensation wouldn't go away. And although this wasn't an erection, his junk seemed to grow with every step he took.

Amanda had called him for a reverse booty call, and GG was more than happy to oblige. He had never been in an apartment so dark before, and while it didn't bother him at the time, he was now suspicious about the countless inverted crosses and pentagrams that decorated her walls, not to mention more burning candles than he'd ever seen before.

But what a good fuck she was. She banged him every which way but loose, and thinking about her made him temporarily forgot about the strange sensations currently running through his dick.

By the time he was five blocks from his pad, his member had grown large enough to rip through his zipper, requiring GG to carry it the rest of the way with both arms as if hauling a coffin.

Somehow GG made it to his apartment with minimal weird stares. His brother Merle was in front of the TV as he jammed something on his unplugged electric guitar.

"We've got problems," GG said.

"What's that?" Merle asked as he looked at GG. He must've been on something stronger than weed, because it took a few minutes for the sight before him to register.

"I said we've got problems." GG let go of his dick, which

he had been holding to his chest since leaving Amanda's. It slammed down on the makeshift coffee table, knocking Merle's ashtray and beer cans to the floor.

Merle stood and pulled his guitar over his shoulder. "What the fuck happened to you?"

"That bitch, that's what happened."

Merle laughed. He pointed at GG's swelled cock and continued to laugh harder. A minute or two passed.

When he didn't calm down, GG said, "Enough already, asshole." His penis, as if on its own accord, swung out and smacked Merle in the side of the head, sending a couple of teeth flying to the carpet. And if GG didn't know better, he'd swear it grew another several inches after making contact with his brother's face.

Merle finally stopped laughing. "Alright! Alright. Take it easy, fuckface." He took a sip from a fallen beer can and spit some blood on the floor. "You mean to tell me banging Amanda caused this?"

"Looks that way," GG said, sitting on the couch. His dick now stretched four feet past his legs and was almost twice as thick as his body.

"Damn. We've gotta do something about this."

"No shit, dickless." GG took the bandana off his head. "Can you get me a beer? My mouth is as dry as shit."

Merle went to the kitchen and returned with a Pabst tall boy. GG drained it in four gulps.

His dick grew even longer and thicker.

Merle sat across from him and gawked.

"Staring at it isn't going to do anything," GG said.

"Shhhh ... I think I've got an idea."

☠☠☠

One of the bouncers dragged an unruly patron through the crowd and out the entrance. When the drunken fool refused to calm down, the bouncer lifted him by the throat and slammed him to the pavement, causing his body to split into countless butterfly-like creatures and sputter away. The line waiting to get in continued talking, unaffected.

When the dismissed patron's friend came out looking for him, the bouncer lifted the rope and allowed two more people to enter.

Merle flicked a cigarette butt halfway across the street. "Everything okay?"

"Everything's fine," the bouncer said, crossing his arms and staring at the endless line of night clubbers.

"Thanks." Merle went back inside after witnessing Joe's method of dealing with trouble and realized he had picked the right man for the job.

Merle made his way through the long, cylindrical club, looking for his brother. The place was packed and he worried they'd run out of beer or whatever mixed drink everyone was sipping. The dance floor in front of the stage was jammed with people grinding up against each other, some having sex standing up as if no one was watching, others laughing, yelling into each other's ears to hear over the deafening mix of punk, techno, and industrial music.

A couple of girls gave Merle the eye, knowing he was the co-owner of this fine establishment, but he kept on, needing to speak with GG. He looked at the ceiling, which dripped with red and white liquid that never seemed to hit the floor. Its dark but fluorescent texture gave the entire place a dim but not painfully dark glow.

Backstage, GG had a small group around him, offering various drugs and whatnots. The Scumfucs weren't due on stage for another half hour, and Merle hoped the fire department wouldn't shut them down before the show, or at least until they sold out of every copy of their latest seven-inch single, although at this point, the cover charge at the door would more than foot the bill for their next few recording sessions.

"So GG," a young woman with spiky green hair asked. "What's the big surprise tonight?"

"You'll have to wait like everyone else," GG said, sticking his hand down the front of her tight jeans. The girl leaned back and enjoyed the probing, continuing to toke a joint.

"Are you done fucking around yet?" Merle hated to interrupt, but business was business. "I gotta talk to you."

He pulled GG away from the girl and noticed the hand that GG had stuffed down her pants was now rainbow-colored. GG sniffed it as he entered the small room they used as an office.

"What's so important?"

Merle lit another smoke and wiped the sweat from his forehead. "In the last half hour the place has expanded by five feet."

"So? Tell Joe we can let more people in."

"That's just it. We'll have to call the Fire Department to change our occupancy sign. If they pull a surprise inspection we'll be fucked."

GG laughed and took his pants off. He stood in black engineer boots, a dirty jock strap, and sleeveless dungaree jacket. "When the fuck did you become such a dick?"

"Someone has to keep things on the up and up around here. If we keep letting things slip we'll be closed down before we know it."

"Will you relax?" GG said as he slid on sunglasses. "Let me get through this gig. Then we'll deal with this bullshit. Okay?"

Merle spit on the floor and took a drag of his cigarette. "Fine."

When GG left to join his band, Merle sat on a ripped old couch they had found in a strip mall parking lot and wondered when the hell he had become so responsible. Perhaps it was when the cash started rolling in just two weeks after they opened the Anarchy Café. Or maybe it was when his brother accepted what had happened to him and decided to deal with shit as long as he could, and so far he seemed to be dealing with things just fine.

Before he could worry any more, one of the walls widened

at least a foot, causing the small room to fill with a salty stench that made Merle gag. *At this rate,* he thought, *this place will take up half of New Hampshire in another month.*

☠☠☠

During the third song of the Scumfucs' set, the green-haired girl from the back room jumped on stage and sang along with GG. Merle laughed from the back of the club, knowing she was in for it. And within seconds GG ripped her shirt off and began fondling her tits.

But the girl was no pushover. As the crowd went wild slam dancing and singing along to "I Wanna Fuck Your Brains Out," she managed to tug down GG's jockstrap.

The crowd quickly became silent, and within a few moments so did the band. The only thing heard was GG's gravely voice until he realized he was the only one making noise.

Merle saw the whole crowd staring at his brother's crotch.

GG looked down.

The topless girl stood with her mouth wide open.

A goat head with red, glowing eyes protruded from where GG's cock should've been. Smoke came from its nose, and Merle could feel the walls of the club expand for the fifth time since they opened a couple hours earlier. This time they seemed to stretch out at least five feet on all sides, pulsing blue veins and barb wire-like hairs jetting out from every inch as morbid decorations. He saw Joe by the entrance admitting more and more people, making Merle wonder if the goat head wasn't somehow communicating with the bouncer and his brother.

As if there was never any silence, the band ripped back into the third verse. The crowd began raping each other, and Merle ran to the front to see what was going on with Joe.

"It's all cool," he said as Merle approached.

"What's all cool?"

"This. The Club. We're kickin' ass." Joe pulled out two stacks of mostly twenties he had shoved in his front pockets. "Must've taken in over five grand already."

Merle shook his head and ran across the street. The Anarchy Café was now taking up three times as much space as they had legal permission to do. The still-expanding right side had crushed a 1981 Pinto. There was blood on the cracked windshield.

As he walked back toward the Cafe, he wondered how long the outside would last until it outgrew the cheap black tarps they had used to cover the exterior "walls."

He also wondered just how long they could keep this going until someone alerted the authorities there was a gigantic dick expanding down South Main Street at an alarming rate.

"Excuse me," someone said as Merle was about to step inside his club.

Fuck.

"Do you work here?"

"Yes. Is there a problem?"

Before the tall fireman could speak, four naked people ran outside and pulled the city official into the club.

Merle ran after them, but the crazed partiers threw the fireman into the slam dancing and raping crowd. As soon as he landed on the floor, everyone turned toward him, their eyes glowing like those of the goat head. The fireman was a big guy, but he was no match for the crowd who held him down and took turns fucking him in the ass. The women shoved their pussies into his face and forced him to chow down.

"No!" Merle cried, but it was too late. When everyone had had their fill, the crowd ripped the fireman apart with their bare hands and threw the pieces into the air, where the moist ceiling seemed to *absorb* the offerings into its system. Its endless veins throbbed, causing the Café to expand yet again.

Shitshitshit. Merle ran to his office, realizing this venture had gone too far. But he quickly found out how wrong he was.

73

"You need to relax, brother." GG appeared in the office even though Merle could still hear the band playing.

"Do you know what just happened?"

"I said *relax*."

The goat head spit a sticky substance into Merle's face. It tasted terrible, but once it slid down his throat he began to unwind. He started to think positively and forgot about the murder that had just occurred in his establishment. He forgot about zoning laws they were violating more and more with each passing minute. And he forgot about the potential lawsuits his raped customers could bring once this mass hysteria ended.

But he realized this *wasn't* mass hysteria. It was the Allin brothers' purpose. It had become their bread and butter and their reason for being.

☠☠☠

Four months after the Anarchy Café opened, it had grown to half the size of New Hampshire. Patrons refused to leave and just when Merle thought they'd have to force people out by any means necessary, the club would expand to accommodate not only the regulars, but curiosity seekers. Club kids and all sorts of nightlife types came from around the globe to get a glance inside the Anarchy Café. Some didn't survive the experience. Some did. And most of the ones who did became permanent fixtures at the club.

By the fifth month, and with *three quarters* of New Hampshire now a gigantic penile nightclub, Merle and GG were approached by the United States Military as well as several men dressed in black suits with dark sunglasses. They were told things had gone off the rails and they needed to cut back.

GG dropped his pants to reveal the goat head, but its glowing eyes and psychic abilities had no affect on the government officials or the mysterious suits. And when they arrived back at the Anarchy Café the next day with a flatbed truck carrying a huge hypodermic needle, Merle saw GG's countenance sag.

"This is courtesy of Uncle Sam," one of the military officers said as two black helicopters lifted the needle from the truck, flew over the club, then dropped it tip-first onto the roof. GG watched in horror as the plunger depressed itself and filled the cock/club with a bubbling purple liquid. There must've been a swimming pool worth of government medicine in there.

GG fell to the floor and screamed. Merle tried to console him but GG involuntarily kicked him in the mouth, causing him to lose a few more teeth.

It took a couple of hours, but the Anarchy Café slowly shrunk back into GG's normal-sized cock. As it did, patrons who refused to leave were crushed to death as others suffocated under the apocalyptic shrinkage. Plenty of people could've escaped, but it was as if the nightclub *owned* them. Both GG and Merle eventually agreed it had been one of the largest mass suicides in American history, although the media, for whatever reason, never picked up on what could've been a truly sensational story.

Blood ran out from the entrance so deep the military had to commission over a dozen septic tank trucks to park outside and suck everything up with their industrial-sized hoses.

Merle slammed his head against a telephone pole as he watched his brother's dick—and their newfound fortune—dwindle down to nothing.

💀💀💀

Two weeks after the Anarchy Cafe's gruesome finale, Merle finally located a doctor down in Manhattan who would be able to re-attach his brother's penis. The goat head had fallen off as soon as the nightclub was injected, and he was sick and tired of watching GG sticking his hand in the hole in his groin.

The operation was a success, although even erect GG was only four inches now, due in large part to the months of abuse as an oversized nightclub and whatever was in the serum the military had come up with to bring it back to normal size.

Upon their return to the mostly flattened New Hampshire, Merle and GG were arrested on several charges, including zoning law violations and endless property damage.

But Merle thought as positively as the now lost goat head had encouraged him to. At least the time they'd spend in jail would be used writing their next several seven inches, and maybe even a full album.

And he knew GG would be plotting a way to get even with Amanda.

THE COPROPHAGUS

David C. Hayes

He had, quite literally, saved the world time and again. He was not the bringer of light. He was the dweller of darkness. He did not forgive and bless and hold the world to his bosom. He was the dark star. The swirling miasma of the universe's piss and vinegar given unto man as a living and breathing mortal latrine and heavy bag, coming only once a millennia to clean the sins of the planet. Reviled, misunderstood and persecuted, he was still absolutely necessary, and when his time on this planet passed, we had to wait… are still waiting… for another of his kind to emerge.

Every welt and bruise on his mortal body shifted the people of the world into the light. He took the punishment that humanity so desperately deserved. He consumed the blackest deeds, forcing them down his throat and allowing the undeserving citizens of the planet absolution. These deeds, these sins, came to him as filth. Piles of steaming, rancid waste matter. Feces and urine. Piss and shit. Vomit and semen and blood. All of it. Every horrible act that every horrible human could devise manifested itself as pain or bodily matter and the savior's task was to shoulder the burden. Eat the pain. Eat the shit. Eat the sin. He was the Sin-Eater.

Like other Sin-Eaters before him, he neither wanted the job nor enjoyed it. The balance of the cosmos was on the line though, and fate dealt him the same hand it had dealt countless other sentient beings over the eons. And, much like those other beings, the people he saved, the members of his species that benefitted from the pain and misery, looked upon him as a pariah. They hated him or, as some have suggested, hated the idea that he had to exist.

This one in particular was reviled by his own people more

than most, but for a very good reason… he made them face their crimes. The abuse that wracked his mortal frame was put on display. Each dripping handful of sin he crammed down his own throat was committed to posterity via late twentieth century technology. If he had to suffer, then they would learn the price of their sins. For the universe gave unto man a thoroughly forgotten son to take their pain and misery onto and into his own self. Born Jesus Christ Allin, he was the Sin-Eater. He was the Coprophagus.

I am Demeter and I have been tasked with telling the story of the Coprophagus' last battle. The one that eventually consumed *him*. As a neophyte in a forgotten order, I am not important, but this record must be made available to the next Sin-Eater and the next. The next Avatar of Putrescence must know of his legacy, that of Allin, greatest among them.

Chosen at birth to shoulder the burden, he spent years under the guise of a musician, showing the young people of the planet what it was he had to do for them. Many misunderstood. Many took the grandiose acts as nothing more than an attempt to shock and destroy the traditional American values they so hotly defended. In the great irony of the Coprophagus, those values were exactly what he had to consume, night after night. The atrocities committed in the name of real Americans pummeled his body from head to foot, breaking bones, tearing skin and rending flesh. Unlike other Sin-Eaters, he gave voice to it.

"Stick me down, step on my face, spit on me. 'Cause I don't scare, you'll see. Make me bleed," he would scream to them from the stage. The young people would dance and punch and kick and cut and slice and stab and he cared not. Every one of them inadvertently provided solace unto the world. Each puncture wound bleeding from the top of Allin's head, mixing with the sweat and tears as it flowed down his chest and onto the stage, edged the world closer into karmic balance. "Gonna do what I want. Fuck you. I don't care what you do to me. Make me bleed."

Analogous to other so-called saviors, whose tiny faiths are measured merely in years and not the age of the cosmos, the Coprophagus would call them to him. All their anger, all their hate and all their violence coalesced, and he allowed them to vent those frustrations on his literal body. Of his flesh. Of his blood. The young people who saw nothing but a bleak future, squandered by their forefathers, took the literal pound of flesh from the Sin-Eater and, without even knowing it, their futures brightened. He would call to them, a singsong of recognition. "Some fuckhead in the corner's getting to me. Talkin` about the way I look and smell. Well I guess he don`t know that I`m the Outlaw Scumfuc. Someone oughta warn him before I knock him straight to Hell."

Humans are despicable though, and, no matter the threshold of pain even the greatest among Coprophagus could endure, the year nineteen hundred and ninety three, by the Roman calendar, proved too much even for Allin. Vile act after vile act, plunging the world itself into a deeper and deeper pit, threatened to overtake the light and forever tip the balance in favor of Chaos. For it is the Lords of Chaos, who existed when the stars were young, that drive corporeal forms into maelstroms. Their need to remake existence in any random image drives them. The Lords of Order have not been heard from since the birth of the planets, yet their Avatar, the Sin-Eater, remains to struggle against the breach. In that year, the year we lost the Sin-Eater, he consumed chaos itself and gave humanity a chance.

As humans are wont to do, and American humans in particular, acts of violence, rage, intolerance, hate, torture, murder, rape, etc. are fairly common. These were the normal sins that the Coprophagus would abolish from the planet. They would build in intensity, from small flesh wounds and bruises and welts covering a multitude of transgressions, to large-scale events akin to genocide and war that required the Sin-Eater to consume the shit and piss and vomit. He needed to make the world whole and that was what he did.

In March of 1992, the Sin-Eater visited the den of the trickster. A media manipulator who sought to turn the public against its own self-interest. The being called "Geraldo" by some was just another agent of chaos. Allin fought valiantly, preserving the truth. He needed to be. He had to be. Without a "him," without a Sin-Eater, they would all be lost because only in that comparison could man feel right about himself. The species knew, even if they refused to admit it, that they were a cowardly, violent lot and had to feel superior to something. The Geraldo only helped to further that cause, which was the price one paid for dealing in chaos... it rarely went as planned. Even in vanquishing the beast, the Sin-Eater was weakened and unprepared for the monumental trials ahead.

January of 1993, the Sri Lanka Navy executed one hundred civilians for no apparent reason. This came on the heels of the dissolution of Czechoslovakia, which brought its own brand of Eastern European barbarism into the world. Fresh off the battle with the puppet of the Lords of Chaos, the Sin-Eater shoveled steaming piles of his own, and others, fecal matter into his mouth. He gagged as it caked his teeth and gums. He could only breathe through his nose and that dried the filth around his lips, causing them to crack and splinter when he cried out, suffering. These sins were heavy.

In February, James Bolger, a cute ten-year-old boy, was abducted, tortured, sexually assaulted and murdered by two other boys. This was the appetizer. A bomb at New York's World Trade Center exploded, killing six and injuring over 1000. His body wracked with pain, taking abuse night after night to wash these hateful, spiteful acts away, the Coprophagus bent backwards and accepted hot, acidic washes of vomit leaving the throats of innumerable donors. Later that month, the United States government raided David Koresh and the Branch Davidian compound. As the Sin-Eater knew, the individual, no matter how depraved, could never hold a candle to what the duly elected or installed or assigned governments of nations could do. That act began a 51 day siege.

The Coprophagus continued balancing the world. His head, split asunder time and again, washed his near naked body in blood, and yet he continued on, despite the pain. He could not ignore it, no being could, but he relished it. The box cutter across the forearm filleted the tissue and muscle, rending the flesh to the bone, gleaming white under the stage lights. The audience cheered... they could not fathom why but they needed this. Their world depended on it. He whispered to them, cooing, "Laying on the floor in a pool of blood and cum. My demons lay beside as I kiss them one by one. Then on that day I met a force that nothing will compare. I was born the son of evil when I fuck the devil there."

March bled into April. Nuclear accidents in Russia, the war in Bosnia raged amid calls of human rights violations, and on the 19th of the month, the Branch Davidians failed to hold against their oppressors. Seventy-six men, women and children were consumed in fire for the sake of their religion, and Chaos chuckled.

The Sin-Eater consumed and consumed and consumed. Hot urine, burning the cuts and welts on his face, streamed over Allin's form as he filled himself with even more shit and piss. The stage was littered with filth as the Coprophagus used the bile of a fan as lubricant and he slipped the large, unwieldy microphone in his rectum. The soft, sensitive skin ripped and bled as the acidic bile stung the open wounds. Yet he needed to press on. Man's inhumanity knew no bounds and he had to be boundless, too. As it ripped and tore and burned, he cried to the heavens, "Pulled out my burning pecker and out came the pus. Though it hurt, but I was devoured by lust. Oh, what a fuck."

May and June rushed toward the Sin-Eater. Reeling from the fire that ate women and children alive, the Bosnian conflagration continued. Lorena Bobbitt sliced her husband's penis off and the Unabomber continued his reign of mail order terror. Pakistani soldiers were massacred in Somalia and IRA bombs destroyed innocent bus riders on the Emerald Isle. Finally, the new President of the United States ordered missiles to be launched in Iraq in retaliation for the assassination plot on his predecessor. The cycle continued.

The Coprophagus took it all in, literally and figuratively. Under the guise of "punk rock," his valiant battle against the Lords of Chaos and their minions raged. His body wracked with abrasions and cuts and tumors and lumps, the Sin-Eater could barely move as he ate sin after sin. The shit of the world filled the gaps in his teeth. Yellow diarrhea caked his mustache.

Barely able to move, let alone actively ingest sins, Allin laid on his back and willed himself to vomit upward. A stomach full of partially digested blood and cum, piss and shit expelled into the air. He closed his eyes as the stomach acid and its contents rained down. He opened his mouth, hoping against hope that this would set the world right, that this act of vileness could redeem the world enough to set the balance straight again.

And it did.

The resiliency of the Coprophagus' human form had reached a limit, but the world reset in that act. Disease filled him. Pestilence embraced him. That last, brilliant act had saved the world one last time. Allin's mortal coil, slipping from his grasp, was only temporary anyway. Like any savior, he knew his time in this existence had a limit. Smiling, the Sin-Eater consumed one last thing and, when he was done, he lay back and waited to stop breathing.

Right before he met the Lords of Order and left the world, there is a story among believers that he eulogized the struggle and sacrifice. On June 28th, barely audible, the Sin-Eater, the Coprophagus, the Avatar of Putrescence, whispered, "Now I`m ready to close my eyes. And now I`m ready to close my mind. And now I`m ready to feel your hand. I`m gonna fuck you now in the burning sands."

I am Demeter and we await the next Sin-Eater. He or she is sorely missed. The years since the time of Allin have proven difficult. The Lords of Chaos have simply waited and allowed the worst in humanity to flourish. There is no balance. There is no one to consume our sins. They are out and open. The world suffers. We suffer.

Still, we wait.

SAN GG

Gabino Iglesias

When it came to The Cuban, only a few things were certain. He was weird as fuck. He had powers that no one at ADX Florence could even begin to fathom. He had three huge pearls underneath the skin of his dick. He loathed every musclehead guard and all other authority figures in the joint. He had no sense of humor.

A strange tattoo of a baldheaded man covered in blood occupied most of his back, surrounded by the words "FUCK YOU" and "SAN GG." The man in the tattoo was naked and crouched on top of a pile of bodies. His bald head was covered in blood and he seemed to be holding a microphone. No one really knew for sure because no one looked at The Cuban for too long or dared get close enough to study the tattoo. Beyond that, everything about The Cuban was a mystery, including his name, age, and anything having to do with his past.

The aura of mystery surrounding The Cuban, as well as the fact that he never smiled or acknowledged a greeting, didn't sit well with the other prisoners. Thus a few inmates had tested him early on. In a place like ADX Florence, which houses the most vile, violent, and dangerous men in the United States Federal Prison System, there were more than a few guys willing to do the testing. Some asked how he'd gotten into the US. The standard reply, delivered without an ounce of humor or sarcasm, was "I rode a dolphin all the way to Miami. Then I fucked that slippery hijueputa's blowhole to death and ate his heart." Others asked how he landed in prison. The response was a stare that could make an Eskimo shiver under his parka while standing in the Libyan Desert at noon.

The first week The Cuban spent at ADX Florence, a gigantic hick by the name of Billy Bob Bobby Joe stopped

The Cuban on the way to the shower and told him he couldn't wait to break himself off a piece of that salty Caribbean ass. The guards found the big redneck's body the next morning, his fuzzy white nutsack stuffed down his throat way past the trachea and his eyeballs somehow intact inside his rectum. They couldn't find his tongue. "All I got is blood for you" had been written in blood on the wall above the bed. The case was never solved because Billy Bob Bobby Joe had been safe, sound, and alone at the last headcount the previous night. In any case, the gruesome death was more than enough to ensure The Cuban wouldn't be messed with again, and it allowed for some pretty wild rumors to start circulating.

Some folks said The Cuban was a shapeshifter. Some days he would appear to be a regular man of about 5' 7" and some days he looked like a seven-foot tall professional bodybuilder who ate Rottweilers for breakfast. Likewise, his black eyes would sometimes turn green or yellow. He could have his head shaved on a Tuesday and then walk out to his shower or show up at chow hall on Friday with a full head of dark curls.

While those changes made everyone fear the man while professing the contrary, what really got to most of the inmates was the voices that would come from The Cuban's cell at night. Sometimes they talked and sometimes they sang or chanted in both English and Spanish. The guards, who were as brutal as the worst inmates, had entered his cell a few times expecting to find someone else in there, but all they ever found was The Cuban sitting on his bed with a dead look in his eyes.

The day all hell broke loose, the inmates were finishing lunch. A huge humanoid thing walked into the chow hall and released a howl that would've made an alpha male wolf piss himself. Every pair of eyes turned to look at the thing. The creature had a greasy mohawk and tiny golden crosses hanging from its ears, which is how everyone identified it immediately as a guard named Henderson.

The thing ran up to a table, grabbed a black inmate with a head full of massive dreadlocks by the neck, lifted him up like he weighed no more than a newborn, and used its other hand to crush his skull. The inmate's eyes popped out with a simultaneous "plop!" that could be heard even above the first few screams from those who had been swallowing tasteless mush a second ago. The monster then used its claw-like nails to remove the top of the inmate's skull, scooped out the man's brain, and stuffed it in its mouth.

The two guards supervising the chow hall stood up and unholstered their weapons. They ran out of their cabin, but one of them, a tall white guy named Johnson who had the biggest biceps many of the prisoners had ever seen, stopped abruptly and dropped his gun. He started shaking as if being electrocuted. His dark brown uniform turned darker in the crotch and then down the left leg as his bladder emptied. The inmates still in the chow hall had to move their heads back and forth between the hulking motherfucker with a mouth full of brains and Johnson, who was still convulsing violently and growing so fast his uniform was being torn to shreds.

Lil Timmy, a dwarf with My Little Pony sleeves covering his arms and a Fu Manchu mustache that reached down way past his chin, looked at The Cuban, who was still sitting down across from him, and shouted, "What the fuck is going on here, man!"

The Cuban didn't know, so he said nothing.

Johnson now resembled a paler, slightly taller clone of the beast that had come into chow hall with a hankering for brains. Both creatures were like slimy, translucent versions of The Hulk with faces that looked like hamburger meat with mouths full of shark teeth. Their bodies had most of the veins running outside the skin and their mounds of muscles pulsed with a life of their own.

The third guard, a mean bastard with no neck named Gonzalez who had pushed The Cuban around every chance he got and called him Tony Montana's faggot brother, dropped to his knees and growled.

Every guard was turning into a monster. Judging by the

way they looked after the transformation, The Cuban didn't have to guess too hard to determine the cause: bad steroids.

There were 429 inmates at ADX Florence and The Cuban knew they had to have at least 50 guards on the premises at all times. If every single motherfucker in the joint had used the same steroids, the problem was going to multiply quickly.

The Cuban looked around. There were only about a dozen stunned inmates in the chow hall with him. The rest had headed back to their cells. Suddenly, being behind really thick iron bars struck everyone as a great idea. The Cuban wasn't about to argue with that sentiment. He stood up and ran.

The cells at ADX Florence were as bare-bones as they come, and The Cuban whispered a "Fuck you" to the powers that be for locking him in a place where nothing could be turned into a weapon when all the guards suddenly transformed into hyper-muscled monsters. Had nobody considered this possibility?

"What the fuck are we gonna do?"

The Cuban looked down and saw Lil Timmy had followed him to his cell. Fear will make a man do inexplicable things, so he wasn't about to ask the little man why he had followed him instead of going to his own cell. He figured that if he was scared, someone a third of his size had to be shitting his pants.

Then he thought about that shit and everything became clear.

What The Cuban was about to do was something that inhabited that weird space between theory and practice. He had all the right words in his head, but he had never summoned San GG, and he didn't have any black candles, which the palero that taught him the ritual had said came in really handy when trying to call forth such a powerful spirit. Also, he had heard that San GG usually manifested in physical form, but he had no idea if even his supernatural strength was enough to bring down the muscled freaks roaming the joint.

An ear-piercing scream that turned into a gurgle was enough to push The Cuban's doubts away. He had nowhere to go, so the summoning was the only viable option. He prayed to his Orishas that Lil Timmy hadn't dropped a deuce recently.

"Are you gonna fucking stand there all day or are we gonna do something, man!?"

Lil Timmy's attitude made what The Cuban had to do a lot easier. The bigger man pushed the dwarf hard. The little man stumbled and fell down on his thick ass. The Cuban reached down, grabbed Lil Timmy by the ankles, and lifted him up.

The little man's ankles fit perfectly in The Cuban's fists, so he inhaled and swung the chubby body against the concrete wall. It sounded like a dead dog hitting the sidewalk after being thrown from the roof a two-story house. It was a sound The Cuban knew very well.

The dwarf's crooked arms went limp, but the groans coming from somewhere deep in his throat made it clear he wasn't dead. The second time The Cuban swung, he gave it all he had, drawing strength from the cold, white fear that was rapidly turning into desperation. Lil Timmy's head cracked like a coconut dropped from a tenth floor window and a thick glop of brains and blood spattered against the wall.

The Cuban dropped the little dead man on the floor and stomped on his stomach a few times to help nature do its thing. After four stomps, the smell of fresh shit reached his nostrils and The Cuban smiled for the first time in a very long time.

Using Lil Timmy's blood, The Cuban drew a pentagram on the floor. In the center of it, he painted a raised middle finger and the words COME FORTH, SCUMFUC around it. Then he pulled the tiny corpse's pants down. He turned Lil Timmy's chunky body around, pulled down his underwear, and used his fingers to collect some of the shit smeared on the dwarf's cheeks. The thick, warm, lumpy mess reminded The Cuban of his mother's awful oatmeal. The only difference was the color and the smell of dead rodent innards that wafted up to his nose.

After surrounding the pentagram with feces, The Cuban started covering himself with blood, which had already stopped gushing out of Lil Timmy's head and was slowly starting to congeal on the floor.

Finally, with the blood covering his head, face, and arms and the shit pentagram in place, The Cuban stood near the center of the pentagram, unzipped his pants, and pulled his dick out. He started rubbing the pearls under his cock skin. They were supposed to be there to give his partners more pleasure, but he'd learned that rubbing them hard also made him cum a lot quicker.

Since he wasn't a fan of jerking it while sitting on the cold metallic toilet or the hard mattress, The Cuban had a decent load stashed in his sack and in less than a minute of rubbing the pearls and tugging, a few white strands shot out. He moved his dick around to make sure he covered as much of the pentagram as possible.

After squeezing the last few drops of cum out of his softening penis, The Cuban tucked himself in and zipped up. Everything was ready to go, and if the screams coming from down the hall were any indication, danger grew nearer by the second. He had to haul ass if he was going to make this thing work.

The croak that came from his throat made The Cuban wonder when he had last spoken to anyone, but he knew he didn't have time to entertain thoughts that didn't have anything to do with the task at hand, so he carried on.

"San GG, deja de clavarte a la muerte y ven a mi. San GG, los que te adoramos y glorificamos necesitamos tu ayuda. Ven a nosotros, San GG, ven ahora."

The mixture of shit and blood surrounding the pentagram began to sizzle and grey smoke came from the raised middle finger.

A dark figure slowly materialized in the center of the pentagram and The Cuban felt his heart skip a few beats, something it hadn't done since he had managed to make that spell work on the dolphin that carried him from the shores of Havana all the way to Miami.

The smell of old sweat and decay grew so strong The Cuban had to close his eyes and hold his breath for a few seconds.

Then it subsided a bit and he looked at the pentagram again. Standing on it was the man he had tattooed on his back, his patron saint, the man he admired most, the being who had transcended the physical world with his energy and anger: San GG.

San GG gazed around, his face contorting into an animalistic sneer as he realized where he was.

"Fuck authority!"

The scream came from somewhere beyond the grave and made the prison walls shake. The Cuban knew he'd done the right thing.

"Some bad pigs are killing inmates, San GG. Can you help us?"

San GG looked at The Cuban and his sneer turned into a deranged smile.

"I say fuck the law. Kill, kill, kill, kill their motherfucking asses!"

San GG hadn't finished saying "asses" when a musclebound freak with a salivating maw full of shark teeth appeared right outside the cell's open door. The Cuban looked at the monster and then at San GG, whose crazy smile had widened even more.

San GG and the overjuiced guard moved toward each other simultaneously. The Cuban had seen videos of San GG when he was alive, fighting folks at shows. Now he witnessed the same ferocity, but coupled with superhuman strength and agility. San GG reached forward and seemed to punch the monster in its gaping mouth, but instead of a punch, he immediately pulled his hand back out, ripping out the monster's spinal cord.

The huge fiend dropped like a squirrel hit with a shotgun blast. San GG walked out of the cell as if on a quest to find a girl he could cut, burn, and then have her piss in his mouth. The Cuban followed.

Two enormous slime balls charged them.

The Cuban knew the smart thing to do and stayed behind

San GG. To his surprise, San GG turned toward him, giving the toothy freaks his back. As they approached, San GG dropped his pants, stepped out of them, and screamed. A massive turd flew out of his ass like a bullet and perforated one of the creature's chests, lifting the creature off its huge feet and dropping it like a trash bag full of old noodles.

The second creature looked at its fallen comrade, roared as it flexed every overdeveloped muscle in its massive body, and ran forward. Again, San GG squeezed out a projectile turd, this time taking the approaching creature's head off.

The Cuban and a very naked San GG made their way down the stairs.

The next creature they came across jumped out at them as they reached the emergency exit stairs, which had been left open when guards had come in and turned into bigger, meaner beasts before getting a chance to close it. San GG jumped up, grabbed its veiny head, and crushed it between his hands. Then he spat on the creature and started mumbling something about his sadistic killing spree.

When they reached the first floor, freedom was something sweet and fluffy The Cuban could already feel dancing on his tongue. The man who never smiled now had a smile plastered on his face that was big enough to rival San GG's maniacal grin.

Two more uber-pumped savages stumbled out of an office about thirty feet from the door. Their legs had gotten so huge they walked like they were trying to keep a horse between their thighs. San GG screamed "It's time to take action, kill the police!" and ran forward.

The hyper-muscled pigs looked confused for a second because they expected the two men to run, not for one of them to come at them, his penis jumping up and down like a small fish out of water. Before they had time to revise their plan, San GG was on them.

With speed that was hard to keep up with, San GG jumped up and landed with his knees on the bowling ball-sized shoulders of the creature on the right. In the blink of an eye, San GG grew a massive erection and used it to stab the creature in the left eye. The Cuban couldn't see everything, but the loud, wet crack that followed informed him that the meat sword had come out the back of the pig's skull. Before that pumped pig's body hit the ground, San GG jumped and landed in the exact same way on the second creature's massive shoulders. The Cuban knew what would follow, so he started running toward the action, freedom the only thing on his mind.

The second creature was dead and on the floor before The Cuban reached them. He almost slipped on the brains leaking out of the gaping hole in the back of the pig's skull, which had landed closer to the door.

Outside, the sun was starting to dip into the horizon. The Cuban knew he had to steal a car and get the hell out of there because Florence was a really small city and more pigs would be on his ass pretty soon. He turned to San GG to ask for just one more favor and saw the man using his fingers to scoop up some of the blood that now covered his body to write something on the wall. Then San GG turned to The Cuban and he could see what his patron saint had written on the wall: 206045.

San GG then cackled madly as his body flickered in and out of this realm. The Cuban mumbled a shy "Gracias, San GG" before turning around to look for a vehicle.

As he ran away from ADX Florence, The Cuban kept repeating the numbers he'd seen under his breath: 206045. As soon as he reached a town and stole some money and clothes, he'd have to add those digits to the ink on his back.

TIPSY MOTHERFUCKER

Joel Kaplan

GG Allin walked through the desert drunk. He wore his usual attire: a filthy jockstrap, combat boots and a train conductor hat. The raw, brutal, rough, and bloody red sun pounded on his pale skin, but he didn't even feel it. Merle had given him a government sunblock SPF 1000 and it seemed to be doing its job. Doing President Bush's dirty work wasn't GG's favorite thing, but it beat fucking the dog.

He'd banged a bunch of heroin before parachuting into Egypt. He nodded off just after jumping out of the plane. GG wasn't afraid to take that final hell ride. He didn't give a fuck. He was the highest power. When he got to hell he'd kiss the devil on the lips. Unfortunately, a bird crashed into him on the way down, and it woke him up in time to pull the ripcord.

He didn't want to fuck this mission up, so he would do everything he could to fuck it up. Self-destructive behavior got his pecker hard as a cast iron pinky. He wanted to fuck himself. He needed adventure. He was a suicidal caveman savant with split personalities and a license to kill for Uncle Sam.

GG squatted down and pushed nice. He pulled out the works he had secreted in his anal cavity and shot up a large needle full of cocaine. He felt better immediately. He threw the empty syringe into the sand. The world was his garbage dump and his trash a holy communion to that old whore mother earth. He walked toward the great pyramid with a greater sense of purpose.

Merle had made him promise to try to get back for a gig he had booked in NYC, so he wanted to wrap this up fast. Caroline and Sue were gonna be there with the usual crew of freaks, faggots, drunks, and junkies, so it was sure to be a real fucking riot.

His jock strap vibrated, indicating an incoming call from his mother. She called him Kevin and went on and on about small town gossip before he told her he loved her and would call her later, "but don't talk to me now." The chatter, chatter, chatter helped the time to pass, but it hadn't really mattered. The great pyramid slowly got bigger as he approached. The sun went down fast, like most of the transsexual hookers GG knew.

As he came upon the pyramid, he heard a familiar patter in the sand: the footsteps of President Ahmed's ninjitsu secret service. They were dressed in the familiar black ninja gear with two exceptions: a blacker than black Ankh on their chests and golden rings on each finger. Each ring was a perfect one-inch tall replica of the great pyramid.

GG followed an old scumfuc tradition and pushed a small bottle of Jim Beam out of his ass and had a swig. It was always happy hour in his asshole. Now he was ready to drink, fight, and fuck with the ninjas.

The three warriors approached and drew their swords. GG gave them the finger while chugging the rest of the Jim Beam. GG knew the ninjas were no match for him when he was hanging out with Jim.

"You should never have come to Egypt, Outlaw Scumfuc. I will kill you myself for Lord Sobek. Now you die," the middle ninja hissed.

"No room for NINJAS!" GG screamed intolerantly and fired at his enemies, with his body as the bullet.

In a sudden flash, GG smashed the glass pint bottle into his challenger's face. The jagged glass tore through the black mask of his assailant, puncturing the eye and drastically slicing the cheek open to reveal the teeth inside. The ninja lost his will to fight and fell to his knees blind, trying to hold his face together. It wasn't working. His mutilated face resembled a rotten jack o'lantern.

"Fuck you GG Allin, you not hardcore," the fallen ninja managed to whisper through his broken face. Spit and blood poured through his cheek with each painful word. In one smooth motion, GG grabbed the katanna from his challenger and kicked him over.

"I'll show you fucking hardcore," GG said in his thick New Hampshire accent, and stomped on the ninja's throat. The vicinity of death fueled the raging fire inside him.

The other two ninjas advanced. GG kicked one in the nuts, but caught a spin kick to the face. Blood dripped down GG's chin. He smiled. This was the chaos he loved. That taste of blood in his mouth was a familiar friend that ignited his bloodlust as much as the whiskey. He spat crimson onto his enemy's face.

"I'm gonna rape you. EAT MY FUCK!" GG screamed at the two remaining foes, spinning the katana.

Despite being ninjas, they were clearly shaken. Their leader had been crushed by this disgusting madman. They backed off to regroup. "Fuck you, GG Allin," one yelled.

"I'm ready, if you're ninja enough," GG said. He bent over and spread his cheeks for the ninjas.

All their years of training had not prepared them for staring into this abyss. They could not avert their gaze from the car accident that was GG's love tunnel. Then the smell hit them like a punch in the dick and they were both immobilized by retching convulsions.

"Say hello to the devil, motherfucker. You can suck my diarrhea," GG yelled and sprayed the guards with a toxic blast of projectile poo from his tuckered out starfish. The feces spray was a biological weapon and it melted the two ninjas into a shit blood soup in the sand. It was pretty, glittering in the moonlight, but it smelled fucking bad.

GG ran into the pyramid. Bush had told him to take out President Ahmed before the ruler of Egypt completed a black magic ritual that would lead to world domination. Bush's presidential panties had been real twisted up about it. He HATED it when anyone else tried to rule the world. GG raced down into the subterranean chamber, following the sounds of chanting.

The Egyptians were so focused on their dark magic, they didn't notice GG enter. The scent of Kyphi incense was overwhelming. President Ahmed stood in front of an ornate altar covered in hieroglyphics. He held a large golden ankh in his left hand.

There was no artificial light in the pyramid, only flickering torches. This added a subtle strobe effect to the ritual. On either side of the president, curvaceous female mummies were bumping and grinding their withered old cloth-covered flesh. From the unseen corners of the chamber, chanting priests rolled in carts full of bound sacrificial victims. They dumped the twenty squirming offerings in the center of the chamber.

Ahmed clapped his hands. Ten immensely muscled and oiled men emerged from the shadows. The men wore only black hoods and loin clothes and carried wicked axes. They proceeded to brutally murder and dismember each offering. Blood and gore flowed freely down the ancient stone trough as axes hacked through the flesh.

Then the blood-splattered killers disappeared. The aroma of death and freshly released internal gasses overpowered the incense.

"Come to us, Lord Sobek," Ahmed screamed.

From one of many secret passageways, a forty-foot crocodile crept into the chamber: Lord Sobek.

Sobek was the first to notice GG, who had been mesmerized by the display of high-level butchery.

Sobek took one look at GG and left as quickly as he had appeared.

President Ahmed looked up, furious at the shit-covered GG. "If this gross drug addicted hobo is the best the USA has to offer, nothing will stop me from completing the ritual!" he exclaimed.

GG's disgusting presence had shattered the purity of the ritual. Ahmed knew if he got rid of GG and re-consecrated the space, he could get Sobek to return for his offering. He lifted his carved staff and pushed a button in the floor.

"A gift for the god of fire and Hell," President Ahmed declared. He had prepared for this contingency.

The wall swung open to GG's left. The unmistakable scent of pussy was so heavy in the air it was palpable. The newly revealed room was full of forty naked women of all ages on their backs masturbating furiously, their legs spread wide. On each of their stomachs was a needle full of heroin. One pregnant drop glistened on every needle tip like pre-cum from Satan's cock.

GG stopped in his tracks, staring at the sea of dripping cunts and needles. Fat pussy, skinny pussy, big clit long lip pussy, pussy of every color and flavor. The sweet nectar flowed free upon the temple floor. GG wanted to stick his tongue inside every one of them, and stick every needle right into his mainline, but he had to finish the mission first.

GG thought of a compromise. He flipped up his jock and got his cock on the loose. He started to beat, beat, beat on it.

President Ahmed laughed. "Soon I will raise Lord Sobek and he will grant untold powers. Egypt will be the most powerful country in the world and all President Bush could do was fly in an anti-social masturbator to watch me in my moment of glory."

GG inhaled the pussy bouquet. It was close to getting him off. The government puppets must be brought down.

"Bite it you scum," GG screamed as he climaxed, took aim and fired.

His small caliber hard candy cock ejaculated five .22 caliber bullets straight into President Ahmed's face, killing the Egyptian president instantly. GG smiled like he had just gummed down a peanut butter sandwich. The girls all jumped up and ran, needles falling everywhere in an opiate rain.

GG grabbed a handful of syringes and charged back outside. They were probably hot shots but he didn't care. No one followed him.

The copter was waiting. He jumped in and shot up.

Dino Sex flew the helicopter to Washington. He had

brightly colored hair and beard and listened to the Lunachicks the whole flight. He landed behind the white house.

GG took off his jock strap. He put on a tiny pair of cutoff shorts and a torn up Nipple Violator shirt. He jumped out of the helicopter and the secret service brought the one man army into the oval office.

"Leave me alone with GG," President Bush said, sitting at his desk. The secret service left.

"Smokes, right now," GG demanded. The president tossed GG a pack.

"Did you do it? Did you kill Ahmed?" President Bush asked while rubbing his nipples. He was very excited.

"Yeah, I killed that motherfucker, and I expect to be compensated the usual way," GG said and lit a smoke. He took off his tiny shorts and lay on the floor naked.

President Bush stood up from his desk, revealing his erection, a twin tiny tower to GG's. It whipped out of Barbara's mouth when he stood and she emerged from underneath the desk, snapping at it like a barracuda on meth.

"GG needs to be paid for saving the world, Barbara, and he likes them old and ugly like you," the President said.

Barbara hiked up her skirt and removed her leather thong, exposing a pubic hairstyle matching her surname. The thick curly hair burst free of her thong like clowns from a clown car. She squatted over GG, who began to happily tongue her musty, cheesy old lady hole after fighting his way through the wiry jungle.

"You're lucky I had all those Mimosas today, GG," Barbara said. She giggled and urinated a thick bright yellow horse stream into GG's eager mouth. The first lady piss made GG's lil cock throb and President Bush dropped to the floor and started sucking it like the solution to the national debt was in GG's balls. GG sucked Barbara's piss-soaked bush and shot a rancid load in President Bush's mouth.

"Time to get the fuck out. Pay me now," GG said as he rolled over.

"OK GG, you don't have to just hit and run. I might need a breath mint. I swear, GG, the consistency of your sperm is exactly halfway between that of a goat and a sick dog. Remember that diseased greyhound we used to have, Barbara? Yuck city, just like that old doggy jizz. C'mon GG, the night is young we could still cuddle up and watch a movie. Barbara will feed you lobster and filet mignon while we watch the Brady Bunch and I lick your balls and asshole, what do you say?" George Bush begged, "I know you love that!"

"I love nothing. Pay me and then I'm gonna leave. I got shit to do. Fuck Alice and the Brady Bunch and your over-enthused rim jobs. You might be the leader of the free world to these other fucking assfaces, Georgie, but you ain't nothing but a dick sucking hole to me," GG said.

George Bush pouted but handed GG the bag full of money and drugs he was owed. The President was familiar with the abuse, and needed it to get off.

GG left the oval office. He was bored with these rich assholes and wanted to get back to the sluts in the city.

Besides, tomorrow was gonna be a big day. He and the Murder Junkies were playing the Gas Station. He was ready for it.

THE SCUMFUCS TOUR TO TOYLAND

Shawn Milazzo

The warm, smiling sun greeted the Scumfucs as they entered Toyland. Happy music notes danced and sang for their arrival.

"What the fuck is this place?" Merle asked, looking beyond his sunglasses, through the rape/tour van's open passenger window.

"How the fuck am I supposed to know?" GG reached from the back seat, slapping his brother on the head.

"Well, we got a fucking show to play here. So keep fucking cool until we get to the damn venue," Killer Kelsie said, not carefully steering the van around the rejoicing music notes.

"Keep cool? Keep fucking cool? I'll show you cool, you motherfucker!" GG grabbed the steering wheel from Killer K. and backseat drove the van over a curb.

The musical notes stopped singing and dove out of the way.

CRASH! The rape/tour van crashed into a cardboard brick building. Pieces of wooden rocking horses, china dolls, spinning tops and other toys that are not fun at all flew in every direction. A sign on the side of the building read: "Where Old Toys Go To Die."

The van sat there smoking for a few seconds. Finally, Merle kicked his jammed door open and stepped out. He took his sunglasses off and threw them back onto the seat. The van's side door slid open. B. Toff, GG, and Killer slowly got out.

"What the hell did you do that for, GG?" Killer K. asked, holding his bloody arm. He pulled off his ripped up T-shirt and bandaged it around the wound.

"Because I fucking can," GG replied.

Merle lit a cheap cigarette and walked around to inspect

the damage on the front end of the vehicle, ignoring the fact that they just destroyed a building. Let alone a building for the elderly. Let alone a building for elderly toys. A contorted metallic tin man was crushed inside the van's grill, silently convulsing.

"I wish Ripp Cord was here. He would know how to fix the engine," B. Toff said, scratching his head.

Merle sneered at B. Toff.

"Well, he isn't 'cuz I ate him," GG said.

"Fuck me, man. The van's fucked," Merle said.

An uninjured marionette with a faded paintjob hopped out of the rubble of the retirement home. "Welcome to Toyland! Everyone has been waiting for the Scumfucs to play this week." He smiled.

CRRRACK. GG ran up to the marionette and punched it, exploding half its head.

"Ah! What did you do that for?!" The marionette lunged backwards, holding what was left of its face.

"You gave me splinters, you fucking doll." GG stepped forward, strangling the marionette with its own strings. "We're going to tear this city down to the fucking ground."

A plastic peg police officer approached the Scumfucs. "Just what do you guys think you are doing, crashing into this building like maniacs?"

"What you going to do about it, pig?" Merle put his cigarette out on the police officer's round face.

An ambulance with a smiley face pulled up to the accident scene. "Is everyone ok?" it asked in a really stupid voice.

B. Toff pulled a liquor bottle out of the van. Killer Kelsie huddled next to him.

"Is everyone ok?" the ambulance asked again in a really stupid voice.

"You won't be!" B. Toff threw the molotov cocktail at the ambulance.

"Hey, I was going to fucking drink that!" GG yelled as the ambulance went up in flames.

101

The ambulance screamed like a schoolgirl. It sporadically drove, searching for the hungry hungry hippo's public pool. It flattened a cat that was walking her litter in a baby carriage. The kittens' last cries happened just before they were squashed underneath the ambulance's tires.

The ambulance's window eyes shattered from the fire's heat. Two gay army men were holding hands shopping when the flaming ambulance rammed into them, melting the couple together.

The Scumfucs passed the helpless police officer back and forth on their cocks, filling him up with semen. They made a random brown anthropomorphic dog drink the semen out of the officer's peg hole.

DING! The creative juices and other juices went off in an imaginary broken light bulb in GG's head.

"Let's fuck the dog next!" GG said.

"Sure. Why not?" Kelsie responded.

The group fucked the dog underneath the crying cotton candy clouds. It began to rain. The police officer cried, the clouds cried, the dog cried. Everyone cried. But the Scumfucs. They laughed.

"Stop! Help! Gooooaaagss!" The dog tried yelling before he was stuffed from both ends.

"I just came up with a new song, guys!" GG yelled, pumping the dog's virgin anus.

"Oh yeah, what's that?" Killer Kelsie asked from the front end.

"Fuckin' the dog!" GG responded.

The group laughed. Not the dog. The dog gurgled in horror.

"Great title! Can't wait to hear you play it later tonight," B. Toff said, piercing the dog's ear hole with his dick and driving it in so far it popped out through the animal's nostril.

The fiery ambulance finally plowed through a toy kid-filled school bus that was waiting for a train to pass, taking some kids with it. The remaining students were trapped inside the school bus, burning alive. The toys made out of stuffing went up in flames the quickest.

SCREEECH. Thomas the train smashed into what was left of the bus. The ambulance continued on its sparking rims rampage.

A shiny royal carriage pulled up to the Scumfucs. Trumpet players came out of nowhere, blasting their tune right into the Scumfucs' ears.

The Scumfucs just stood there wondering what the hell was going on. One of the trumpet players blew his trumpet on a high note and a massive umbrella opened above. A colorful midget man with licorice candy hair and gumball buttons stepped off the carriage to greet the group.

"We must be in England or some shit," Merle said.

While the Scumfucs were distracted, the dog held his butthole and ran away.

ZAP! Lightning shot down from the cotton candy clouds and struck the retreating dog. His anus fell out as he pissed and shit all over the side of the road. Citizens of Toyland that saw the tragedy cried. The Scumfucs laughed.

"Welcome to Toyland!" the midget said, twirling his hand and bowing.

"Who the fuck are you?" GG asked.

"Why, I am the Great King's announcer. You must be the Scumfucs, I presume," the weird looking midget said.

"Where can I find the Queen of England?" GG asked. "I want to fuck her,"

"Heh heh. The king's daughter said you guys would be the chatty type. Please jump aboard." The announcer pointed to the carriage.

"Hold up, I need to get my drugs." GG turned to the van.

"What about our fucking instruments?" B. Toff asked.

"Don't worry about that. We'll have them delivered by the Great King's royal deliverers," the midget said.

Killer Kelsie shoved the candy midget fuck. "No one's touching my fucking guitar, asshole."

The announcer put his hands up. "Please, I don't want any trouble. Climb aboard."

"Yeah, and this city is going to pay for the damage to our van," Merle stated.

"Don't worry. You will all be paid handsomely for playing in Toyland." The midget smiled.

Merle pulled a glass tube out of his pocket. He packed a tiny white rock in it and put his lighter to it. The solid rock boiled into a liquid, and then evaporated as a gas. He passed it to Killer Kelsie, who hit the other end of the pipe. The band's eyes lit up, either from the crack they were smoking or from the last statement by the announcer. Most likely, both.

"Hey, they have violated the law of code 33," the deflowered police officer said as he crawled to the announcer.

"Shut the fuck up." GG stepped on the officer's head. It exploded.

The band climbed into the carriage.

"Got the drugs!" GG said.

The sky cleared up and the sun came back out as the carriage took the band on a tour of Toyland. A jack in the box popped up to direct traffic at the intersections. Apples and Bananas crossed streets. Block men construction workers slid on chutes and climbed up ladders, working on Lego buildings downtown. Barbie purchased a vehicle with Ken at a busy toy car lot, while cars were honking to a musical tune. Detectives practiced their skills at the police station on Guess Who. Decks of cards played poker against each other in a cafe. Stuffed squirrels ran up trees to feed families of happy angry birds. Army men practiced simulated combat exercises with G.I. Joes.

The carriage went up lively bouncing mountains. Near the forest was a huge sawmill where Lincoln logs were prepared for shipment via train set. They were getting closer to the Great King's castle.

"And here you can see..."

"Wherrrre are the whorrrrres?" GG interrupted, falling back and forth in a heroin induced stupor.

"Yeah, we need some bitches up in here," B. Toff explained.

"Too much cock." Merle flicked a cigarette out the carriage window.

A forest fire erupted, killing a whole bunch of tiny toy animals. A mother rabbit hopped out of the burning woods, coughing up smoke and black flakes of charred lung. She forgot her young who were now engulfed in flames. Smokey the bear tripped on his shovel and his intestines spilled out. Lincoln logs fell onto loggers, crushing them.

BOOM! The sawmill exploded for no apparent reason. A few workers ran out screaming, on fire, shards of glass stuck into them. Coiled branches perforated already tool-impaled bystanders. Other workers barely limped or crawled out with saw blades halfway in them, jetting blood and gore everywhere. A melting plastic pig dipped his gooey head into gasoline, thinking it was water.

"Oops," Merle said.

A standing survivor wiped his head in relief at being left unscathed. The burning, sparking-rimmed ambulance collided into him.

Billowing smoke from the forest fire caused combat drones to malfunction above the military exercises. The drones deployed bombs onto soldiers, thinking they were the enemy. It looked like a real war.

G.I. Joes exploded, making their fingers pull the trigger on their weapons. The bullets chopped up hundreds of army men and archers released arrows into a crowd of travelling nuns. A destroyed army man holding a grenade released the safety. His upper body dropped into a medieval catapult. The catapult artillery operator knight was being branded by his own armor from intense heat. The catapult launched the torso of the army man to the city. The grenade rolled toward a propane tank next to the Lego construction.

Humpty Dumpty sat on a wall. Humpty Dumpty had a great fall. Flies laid eggs on top of Humpty Dumpty. Poisoned crows pecked at his yoke insides. They shat maggots all over pedestrians after they were done. Buildings came down. Civilians of Toyland screamed in terror. Sick children puked on each other.

Rubble, chemical weapons and debris decimated half the city.

The carriage continued up the mountain.

"Where the fuckkkk is the Queen of Englandddd? I want to rip her oppppen," GG said.

"The Queen of England does not live in Toyland, sir," the announcer responded.

"You look like you taste good." B. Toff tore off one of the announcer's candy ears.

"Oww! What are you doing?" the announcer cried.

"What are you made out of, you stupid little man?" Kelsie pulled the syringe out of GG's dick. He stuck it in the announcer's arm and extracted candy liquid out of his veins.

"Give me that." GG grabbed the used syringe. He injected the man's fluids into his arm.

GG's kaleidoscope eyes lit up from the candy midget man's drug. He stood up in a crazed frenzy. He crashed through the carriage's side, tucked, rolled and ran toward the castle.

"I feel faint." The announcer rested his head on Killer Kelsie.

"Get the fuck off me," K. said, slamming the announcer's head into the carriage.

The magnificent castle had a clean moat around it. The drawbridge was pulled up, awaiting the arrival of the Scumfucs. GG Allin leaped across the moat and crashed through the entrance of the castle. The guards tried to stop him. GG broke their plastic bones and continued destroying everything and everyone in his path.

Merle stuck his head out of the broken carriage. "Hey, weird looking drivers, just take us to the damn venue."

"As you wish, sir." The carriage slowed down to turn around.

"But you haven't properly met our king," the announcer said.

"We don't bow to anyone," B. Toff responded, kicking the announcer out of the carriage. The midget bounced down the mountainside, to his death.

They believed.

The carriage went back to the city's venue.

In the middle of the road was the announcer, barely breathing. A candy cane spinal cord stuck out of his broken neck, having rolled all the way down the mountain to land in front of the venue just in time for the Scumfucs' arrival, sans rampaging GG. The carriage drivers must not have seen the announcer though. They ran over him. Liquid candy oozed out of the announcer's head.

☠☠☠

I'm going to jump off this goddamned tower, GG thought as he ran up one of the castle's spiral staircases. He didn't notice the mysterious glowing hooded feminine figure watching him from afar. He was too fucked up from the candy's psychedelic reaction.

GG reached the top of the tower and looked out onto Toyland. Puff, the magic dragon, was gliding in the sky, leaving sparkling rainbow trails behind.

Puff flew over to GG. "I don't think I ever saw you in Toyland before. What's your name?"

Puff, the Magic Dragon met by GG,
who frolicked in the autumn piss in a land converted by GG.
Little Jackie Paper loved that dragon Puff,
but GG rolled Little Jackie Paper and made that dragon huff.
Together they would travel on a boat with a billowed sail,
GG snorted coke off of Puff's gigantic tail.
Noble kings and princesses would bow whene'r they came,
which was a lot for GG when Puff roared out his name.

107

💀💀💀

"Uhhh, are we at a carnival or something?" B. Toff asked, back at the venue.

"Yeah, this doesn't look like the shit shacks we're used to playing in," Merle added.

The Scumfucs got out of the carriage. The front of the building was overly colorful and plastic, with a "Closed" sign in the front window. Posers, curious citizens, and groupies wrapped around the building, patiently waiting for the doors to open. The Scumfucs ignored the screaming fans at the crowded entrance, shoving them out of the way as they went inside.

The concert hall was well lit, decorated with picture frames of toy celebrities who had appeared there in the past. For how big the building was on the outside, it was quite small on the inside.

In the middle of the stage was a giant statue of the King of Toyland. The statue took up most of the stage, nearly touching the ceiling. If the statue resembled the king at all, he was overweight, concealing possible balding from his crown, and pretty much the spitting image of Santa Claus. He was valiantly holding a scepter, and it looked more like Lenin monumental propaganda from the Soviet Union than anything else.

"What the hell is this?" Killer Kelsie threw up his arms.

"It's taking up half the stage," B. Toff said.

"How the fuck are we supposed to play a fucking show with this fucking thing on the fucking stage?" Merle asked.

"At least our equipment was already set up by the, uhh, what did that short guy call them?" B. Toff asked.

"Slaves," Merle answered.

"Yeah, the slaves," B. Toff repeated.

An accordion arm with a white Mickey Mouse glove reached from the front of the concert hall. The hand flipped the sign to "Open" and then disappeared back inside the wall. Fireworks exploded high above the building. The toys and animals danced around the toy structure. The club doors flung open, dispersing confetti and glitter everywhere. The people of Toyland skipped into the building. It looked like a child's fucking birthday party, not a punk rock show.

The group jumped on stage and adjusted their instruments. There was no sound guy. It was just a sentient machine beeping and flashing behind a short wall. It was off to the side, close to the entrance.

A mysterious hooded female stood in the middle of the crowd.

GG better show up. I'm his biggest fan! Dahlia lowered her cowl. Even though she slightly glowed, the citizens of Toyland didn't notice the Great King's daughter standing in their midst.

But The Scumfucs did, they definitely noticed the royal meat sock. Well, their dicks did anyway. The toys were too busy staring up at the stage in anticipation, half of them not knowing that the frontman wasn't even there. Unbeknownst to the Scumfucs, the princess was the reason they were playing Toyland that night.

B. Toff leaned over his drums and whispered to K, "Goddamn, you see that piece of ass right there?"

"Indeed I do!" Killer K. dropped his tongue.

"GG would love her? Where the fuck is he?" Merle asked.

💀💀💀

A dragon lives forever, but not so little boys,
Spray-painted wings and giant cock rings make way for other toys.
One gray evening it happened, GG crashed through the venue,
and Puff, that mighty dragon, asked what drugs were on the menu.

The venue's roof collapsed. Panic spread through the building. Puff, the Druggie Dragon, landed on the Great King's statue. GG slid off Puff, slamming his face onto the stage.

Merle picked his brother up.

GG grabbed the microphone off the stand. "You guys ready for some fucking noise?!"

The speakers were broken so The Scumfucs just plugged into Puff, the Druggie Dragon's butt. The band's rebellious music blasted through Puff's mouth like a protest through a megaphone.

The Scumfucs didn't even get to play a third of a set before the toys mutated into overly violent punk rockers. Most of them shed their original plastic skin or fur. Maybe it was the drug infused shit GG threw at the crowd. Maybe it was the hypnotic guitar noise. Maybe it was from B. Toff blasting away at his drums. Or maybe it was Puff, the Druggie Dragon, burning the fucking place to the ground. Whatever it was, it caused the toys to overthrow the Great King's rule over Toyland.

💀💀💀

Anarchy was everywhere in the streets.

A massive toy orgy began at what was left of the venue, and the Scumfucs were at the center of it, all except GG.

Punk toys had stolen him away. They carried GG Allin upside down on a crucifix. Jesus was written in blood on GG's stomach.

Toys threw rocks at shop windows, looting everything. Jean jackets, spikes and multicolored hair was everywhere. The mob pulled apart a robot who was trying to maintain order in the streets. His oil sprayed when they finally beat him down with baseball bats and chains. Cars were stomped on. Barbie dolls were raped.

"Drink, fight and fuck! Drink, fight and fuck! Drink, fight and fuck!" the toys chanted, closing in on the Great King's castle.

"GG!" Dahlia cried out from the mob.

"Huh?" he asked, upside down.

The princess ran over to him. "I'm going to peel you off of that crucifix."

RRIPP! "Cunt, what did you do that for?" GG asked.

"There's no time to explain! Come, we must go through the secret passageway to the castle." Dahlia grabbed GG by the bloody hand and pulled him into an alley.

I'm going to fuck this little girl, GG thought.

💀💀💀

Twenty-Three Minutes Later...

SLAM! The Great King of Toyland slammed the glittery magenta door behind him, taking refuge in the castle from the mob outside. The rebellious toys closed in. Hot sweat dripped from the Great King's forehead as he shook in absolute terror, his broken crown forgotten. His two loyal toy soldiers stepped back, their swords raised in the direction of the chaos.

SSSSSSSSSSS. A watery noise slapped against something meaty. A gurgling sound came from deeper in the castle, from the princess's bedroom.

The king and the soldiers followed the sound, ready for anything.

They thought.

Standing above GG Allin was Dahlia, the Great King's daughter. She was pissing inside GG's mouth, mostly missing and splashing on the crack lighter-burned, bloodstained bed sheets. The urine trailed from GG's overflowing mouth to the broken liquor bottle he was inserting in the punk baby doll's orifices.

The morning before, she had been a beautiful, untouched girl, brushing her long golden hair at her luxurious vanity. She had been the epitome of pedophiliac lust, the essence of purity. On this fucked up night, after her perverted transformation, most wouldn't have been able to recognize her.

But the Great King did.

Her room had changed as well. Her pink wallpaper was torn, shat on and pressed together like a Play-Doh compression machine, much like her cunt hole. The chipping, jaundice-skinned doll lifted her plaid, pleated mini-skirt with one hand, exposing her gaping train tracks.

Shocked, the king stared at the abomination that was once his daughter. Black fingernails were attached to shaking hands and arms that were busy tying off with some type of rubber tubing. The uncontrollable giggling skag was shooting up skag smuggled from Mexico in the assholes of children mules. The princess's rotted teeth clenched the rubber tubing in her dripping cum dumpster mouth. Her makeup was smeared with sins and mental scars that no one should endure. A crafty hair stylist had shaved the sides of her head, missing spots, and put her hair up in a mohawk streaked in viral excrement.

"Piss in my mouth, you dirty fuck whore," GG said.

The room was trashed and pretty much looked like a New York dumpster in a dirty infected prostitute alley inhabited with regurgitated sewage from a manhole, if gravity reversed. Severed toy limbs wrapped in cute kiddy wrapping paper dangled from chicken wire, some still twitching. Made-up toy torsos decorated the room. Their jaws snapped out muted screams, their vocal chord stuffing strewn about. On the floor was a little dipping bird frowning as he tapped, tapped, tapped a bound porcelain sailor boy, cracking his wide eye open.

GG sat up and turned toward the astonished Great King. He sloshed the little girl's pee pee around inside his mouth and spat it at the king's face.

GG jumped off the bed and beat the living toy shit out of the toy soldiers. He disarmed the first and skewered the other with the sword. Then he pointed the sword at the king, inching closer to him.

"P-please. Don't hurt my daughter, Dahlia," the king pleaded.

"Get on your knees, you faggot," GG said.

The king complied.

"Now, open your fucking mouth," GG said.

GG whipped his limp cock out of his underwear. It didn't stay limp after it entered the Great King's precious, pretty lips.

The king sucked with dedicated precision, back and forth, back and forth.

The king's eyes bulged when GG's sticky man juice shot to the back of his throat. He choked, backing away. The king gasped for air. The semen made a cum bubble in his mouth. GG thrust his hips forward, forcing his cock back into the king's fuck hole. He urinated inside the king.

Spent, GG decapitated the king with the sword, severing his own penis in the process. He ran at the bedroom's stained glass window and crashed through it.

"I told you motherfuckers I was going to commit suicide!" GG yelled on his way down.

THE ULTIMATE SHOCK

Airika Sneve

"How are your skin tags?"

"Still bleeding from the last show. I just had two hundred put on last week."

"I forgot about your stupid skin tag operation. Most people pay to get those things taken *off*."

"Not me. I'm GG Allin, and I am a religious. Fuckin'. Experience."

Perched on a back-alley milk crate in nothing but stained tighty-whiteys, GG glared at his shaggy haired, tattooed brother-slash-Murder-Junkies-bass player. He ashed his cigarette between two scabby white knees. The day was cloudy but hot. The wind tickled his nipple hair.

With a stitch in his brow, he puffed twin jets of smoke through his nostrils and watched a group of crust punks unloading amplifiers from a purple van in the alley behind the club.

"I'll do whatever it takes to do what's never been done. We fucking need it," said GG. He blew smoke out the side of his mustachioed mouth. "The show's getting stale, man. I need to find the ultimate shock."

"*What*? You're the craziest fucker alive. Rolling in broken glass. Eating your own shit. Flinging shit at the audience. Beating up guys *and* their girlfriends. Hell, man, *skin tags*. No one does that."

"Same old shtick I've been doing for years." GG ground his cigarette out and flicked it violently against the wall. "How much longer are people gonna keep showing up for it? Once they've seen it all, what's left?"

"They'll keep coming."

"Bullshit. People will get tired of it, and then what? Putter all over the U.S. in a van with no muffler and no heat playing basements for beer?"

"What's wrong with that?" Merle glugged the last of his PBR. He belched, crushed the can, and tossed it into the alley. GG kept his eyes glued to the band hauling half stacks like ants carrying cookie crumbs.

"That's not a rush," said GG "That's getting old and predictable. Legacy *over*." His dirty nails scrabbled at his head, its pasty baldscape textured by a braille map of scars, cuts, and gashes.

"You worry too much. Always have."

"This shit is wearing thin. I need to find the ultimate shock, or it's all over."

A towering figure in black leather pants with a Herculean chest bound by a leather vest exposing thick, hirsute arms, leapt out of the van, throwing a shadow like a great Greek column. It whipped its blue-black mane over its shoulder like a lizard tail, then hoisted an enormous guitar cab on its back and sailed toward the club like a grade-schooler toting a backpack.

GG's and Merle's eyes widened. There was no mistaking the amber eyes, the furrowed snout, the jigsaw jags of teeth.

"A werewolf," breathed Merle. "I'll be dipped in beer-battered shit."

GG doubled back, his eyes narrowed. "Those things are only supposed to be in *deep* terrain, aren't they? Like Lithuania? Transylvania? Anywhere with an *ania*?"

The werewolf caught GG's eye. Their gazes clashed like swords. Or lightning.

Merle snorted. "This is Bumfuck, Wisconsin. How much more deep woods can you get?"

"I guess. Those things were discovered in the Montana wilderness, weren't they? Have we been to Montana?"

"Probably. Werewolves have been known for what, ten years now? Ain't you ever seen one close-up?"

"No. Have you?"

Merle paused. "No."

"Can they turn people into werewolves?"

"There's never been a documented case."

115

"You never really hear about 'em killing people, do you?"

"Not often, but when they do…"

The werewolf returned to the van. The other guys piled heavy drum gear high into its arms like steel kindling.

A slow grin seeped over GG's face like spreading ink. Or blood.

"*The ultimate shock*," he whispered.

Merle eyed him warily. "Whatever it is you're thinking, stop."

GG picked up an empty beer bottle and tapped it dreamily against his palm.

"GG, I don't like the way your eyes are shinin'. The last time they shined like that, we ended up in some freaky writer's cellar playing pin-the-tail-on-the-asshole. With rail spikes."

The werewolf loped toward the club, arms piled high. GG hurled the bottle and hit the creature square in the shoulder. It snarled and whipped its huge, heavy head GG's way.

It didn't drop a single drum.

"*Holy fuck!*" Merle flattened himself against the wall. His eyes trained on the beast, he felt around for large rocks, pipes, anything remotely lethal.

"Hey shit-for-brains!" rasped GG "I got a question for you!"

"*Shut up!*" Merle hissed.

The werewolf snorted, its eyes spitting sparks.

GG thrust his chin high, higher, higher still until it angled at the creature's face. It had to be at least eight feet tall. Merle swore under his breath—or prayed. GG's trademark rasp shot out as brusquely commanding as ever.

"Why the fuck are you wearing an Exploited vest?"

The werewolf answered in a low, guttural voice. "Because Wattie could kick your shitstained ass drunk and blind-folded."

"Really." GG nodded slowly. "What's your name." A command, not a question.

"Nebemakhet."

Nebemakhet's buddies smirked at GG with folded arms and amused sneers.

"Neba-whatever-the-hell. You in the band?" asked GG calmly.

"I'm the singer." Their eyes clashed.

"What're you guys called?"

"Pantheon."

"Well, Nebemakhet of Pantheon, after your set, you fucking fight me. Onstage. *To the death.*"

Merle choked. GG stared defiantly as the crust punks in Pantheon hooted in mocking disbelief. Finally, Nebemakhet gave a sharklike grin and what looked like a nod before leaping into the back of the van for more gear.

"That look like a yes to you, Merle?" asked GG

"Fuckin' A, now you've done it."

"The ultimate shock. I told you, I finally figured it out."

"You're gonna do what you want, regardless of what I say."

GG picked off a skin tag and flicked it into the alley with one bloody fingertip. Nebemakhet emerged from the van with a bass drum in one hand and a hundred pounds of cymbals in the other. He whirled into the club without a glance.

"Fight to the death," GG said almost tonelessly.

Merle shrugged, emitted a lengthy sigh, and farted.

☠☠☠

"You want to *what?*" barked a mohawked, pimple-faced guy with a half-smoked roach tucked behind his ear.

"You heard me, Starkey," GG replied. "I'm gonna fight that werewolf to the death onstage tonight. We need at least two more hours. I want to get fucking *everyone* here. Even the hardcore basement junkies will crawl out of their holes for this."

"I dunno, I already told everyone seven," said Starkey.

"Tell 'em nine. They'll wait." GG balled his fists. Breathing deeply, he relaxed them. "We're about to make underground history, and you can be a part of it. Your choice."

Starkey considered. "Vag-Ass," he said, signaling to a diminutive punk messing with the stage lights. "The show starts at nine."

"Nine? I thought—"

"Take the van, hit the streets, spread the word. Tonight, GG and the werewolf fight to the death onstage."

"*What?*"

"Do it. Go."

Badly-lined eyes wide, Vag-Ass nodded and raced out the door.

"You better not be puttin' one over on me," said Starkey. "You get nothing if you are. No blow. Nada."

"If I'm snorting blow with you at the end of the night, I really am the messiah."

"Oh, brother," said Merle, slinging his bass over his shoulder.

GG nodded with a steely gaze. "Two hours 'til we hit the stage, four 'til the fight. Let's gear up. It's on."

☠☠☠

GG and Merle spent the next hour-and-a-half running around like dickless chickens. The shitstorm had hit. GG fielded breathless questions from all directions. The crowd swelled from a trickle to a surge. The word was out: tonight, GG would either kill or be killed—by a werewolf—onstage.

It was brilliant, even better than onstage suicide (which GG had threatened numerous times). It was the ultimate shock.

Together—huddled backstage while Pantheon laid low in their van—Merle, GG and Starkey concocted a simple but effective battle plan: a silver grommet belt. Silver was the only substance known to kill werewolves, in the rare instance they attacked.

GG also stuffed a jack knife in each boot for good measure.

It seemed everyone in the punk rock community had something to contribute. One guy provided the pyramid-studded battle belt. Someone else brought wood glue, and with it they stuck everything they could think of onto the belt. Since the belt itself was studded with cheap metal, they relied on silver jewelry to adorn it. People came with offerings of silver rings, handfuls of pubic hair, fingernails, broken glass, and boogers.

They called this work of art the Booger Belt.

During the hustle and bustle, GG got an education in Wisconsin werewolves from the locals. It turned out werewolves were scarce in this part of the state, and Pantheon were out-of-towners. Wisconsinites occasionally saw werewolves wander into taverns, or at the hardware store, and some even worked fringe jobs like warehousing. Though scarce and generally peaceable, they were deeply mistrusted.

GG, Merle, and the other Murder Junkies huddled in a circle. Nebemakhet and his band sat at a nearby table, grinning over mugs of lager. The beast's amber eyes flashed at GG like a penny in the moonlight.

GG swallowed hard. "All that silver on the belt's real, ain't it?"

"Yeah, yeah, everyone swears," said Vag-Ass, nodding rapidly.

"It better be, or you're dead," said Merle.

A shiver snaked up GG's skin tag-stippled spine. He had a Booger Belt, and jack knives to boot. What was there to worry about?

"Good," he stated. He hoped no one noticed the quaver in his voice.

☠☠☠

One hour until showtime.

GG and the Murder Junkies were on first, Pantheon would play second, and then the final fight was on.

"You think he's gonna go through with it, Merle?" asked GG, peeking through the curtain backstage at the restless crowd.

"Are *you?*"

"Fuck yeah! I'm the messiah! *I fear nothing!*" GG raked his fingernails down his chest and reopened scratches from two stages ago.

"Can I have your choker when he rips you apart?"

"Ain't gonna happen," growled GG. "Vag-Ass!"

The little punker hustled up to him with huge lemur eyes.

GG peeked behind the shabby curtain. "How many people are out there? A hundred?"

"We'll have double that by showtime," said Vag-Ass. "I've still got a few doors to knock on."

GG saw his legacy looming large and fearsome before him. This was it; he knew he couldn't be young and dangerous forever. The time had come to seal his legend as the most dangerous musician of all time. Whether he bled the wolf, or the wolf bled him, he would go down in rock 'n' roll history.

GG searched for Nebemakhet, but the beast was nowhere to be seen.

He popped a laxative and clutched the silver booger belt.

Forty-five minutes to showtime.

☠☠☠

The Murder Junkies were up.

The stage lights popped on and the band ripped into gear, tearing through their set like a grinding, clashing punk rock train gone off the rails.

GG unclamped his butt cheeks and unleashed a torrent of diarrhea upon the crowd. He broke a bottle over someone's head and raked the shards over his body. He plucked off skin tags and flicked them into people's faces.

GG strutted, roared, crapped, and preened naked and bleeding, but his mind was elsewhere. Throughout the butt-drag through razor blades that was "Sleeping In My Piss," he searched the sea of faces jeering and bobbing like a fever dream, but the snarling face with the blue-black mane was not there.

The set concluded and the Murder Junkies swept their shit off the stage, and still Nebemakhet was nowhere to be found. With sweat-stung eyes, GG watched the stage as Pantheon assumed their places. The spotlight swung to the mic stand.

Nebemakhet appeared as if under the transparent light of a full moon.

GG's anus clenched.

💀💀💀

Throughout the set, the beast arched and prowled and screamed and howled. The crowd went insane. The music was fearsome, tribal, frightening. Nebemakhet was otherworldly, and when his eyes found GG's, GG's already-emptied bowels emitted a single puff of air.

The next half hour went by in a blur, and then the music died away to a chorus of applause.

GG clutched the booger belt.

The fight was on.

💀💀💀

"L-ladies and gentleman!" squawked Vag-Ass in the middle of the stage. "The moment you've all crawled out of your shitty, pot-smelling basements for! The great GG Allin and the wicked werewolf Nebemakhet face off until one of them bites the almighty biscuit! ARE YOU READY?"

Applause thundered like a mountain storm. GG stepped onstage. He faced Nebemakhet.

"Tear him apart, GG!" someone shouted.

A girl in shiny pink Doc Martens yelled, "Rip his asshole out!"

121

GG clutched the booger belt.

Nebemakhet held nothing.

GG snapped the belt like a whip. Nebemakhet's yellow eyes flickered over the weapon, then at GG. He grinned.

"And now!" squealed Vag-Ass. "FIGHT!"

The stage lights felt very hot on GG's scalp. If the hairy-ass werewolf was melting too, it didn't show it.

They circled each other. The crowd pumped tattooed fists and hollered. This was his legacy; GG knew he had to succeed, or die trying. With a mighty war cry, he whipped the belt at Nebemakhet. The werewolf twisted nimbly aside.

"Come on, fleabag! You scared?" GG said, snapping the belt. "Eat silver!"

"You don't know what you're getting into," Nebemakhet snarled.

The werewolf rushed at GG. GG kicked out and yelled, but Nebemakhet flashed around him to the side of the stage.

He had made a fool out of GG Allin, resident punk rock messiah, and the grin on his snout showed he knew it.

Rage boiled up through GG's rectum to the top of his greasy pate, infusing him with molten determination.

He was the messiah. He would triumph.

GG shouldered sweat off his brow. He gripped the booger belt until his hands stopped shaking.

GG stood squarely in the center of the stage. The audience raged. GG looked into their faces, and he knew: they wanted blood, and they didn't care whose.

They just wanted to see someone bite it.

Nebemakhet barreled toward GG and, again, whirled away at the last second. GG spun around, almost losing his balance. His belt lashed empty air.

The audience was laughing.

GG swore to himself that if he survived, he was going to skin every one of their asses twice.

Nebemakhet played to the crowd like an expert showman. He sneered and bared his razor fangs, showboating like a WWE villain.

GG plowed toward Nebemakhet and heaved a foot at him. The werewolf jumped aside. The crowd went nuts.

GG faced Nebemakhet, panting. The blasted thing grinned at him, taunted him.

His blood boiled. He was going to kill this fucking were-wolf if it was the last thing he did.

Nebemakhet mocked GG with more of his wrestler showboating. GG had taken an extra laxative, hoping to expel werewolf-tripping anal spray, but when he squeezed, all that emerged was a hard-packed nugget. Nebemakhet kicked it nimbly out of GG's asshole.

Nebemakhet turned to the audience, goading.

GG charged. This was his moment.

He snapped his belt into the beast's ribcage. Nebemakhet snarled and clutched where the belt had struck. It looked from its bloody fingers back to GG

Nebemakhet charged, roaring and punching out the stage lights in its path. GG readied the belt.

The stage lights blasted out one by one.

GG and the werewolf collided.

An overzealous drunk punk crashed his too-tall skullet into the room's only light bulb, and it shattered.

The room went dark.

💀💀💀

Vag-Ass swept up the last of the light bulb glass. The crowd had cleared, and now there was nothing but a ragtag group of staff and hangers-on milling and cleaning up the aftermath.

The stage was covered in blood.

Two punk girls scrubbed the stage. Starkey sat at a rickety high top table, staring into space.

The purple van had departed.

Merle slumped on the stage next to the single bloody butt cheek under the restored spotlight. The glute was all that was left of his brother. Grimacing, a punk girl held up a broom and dustpan.

"Give me a minute," Merle said.

The girl clomped off in her Doc Martens. "GG's dead, dude," she said. "I knew that thing was gonna slaughter him!"

"It would've been more intense with the lights on," said her friend.

"At least there's not much to clean," smirked the girl with a glance at the ragged butt cheek next to Merle.

"Shut the fuck up and show some respect," he said.

Wordlessly, Vag-Ass clapped a hand on Merle's back and handed him an eightball of coke. Merle pocketed it and patted the crimson-washed glute.

His eyes behind his dark sunglasses were dry and serene, for he had glimpsed something no one else had: not one, but two werewolves left the club that night. It wasn't the butt cheek that was missing GG; it was GG who was missing the butt cheek.

Apparently, werewolves could convert people after all.

From that day on, if you happened to pass a road-worn purple van, and you listened closely past the wind and the shifting notes of trees, highway and the restless night, you might just hear a raspy voice howling strains to "Suck My Ass it Smells."

GG Allin had finally found the ultimate shock.

RASHES IN THE SCREAM

Nicholaus Patnaude

Cheryl and I wanted to see the spectacle of GG Allin bleeding and slinging his enema-induced feces, but Woeselly Prep was a dignified, cultivated environment and, as teachers there, we were meant to exemplify an airtight moral purity.

We'd heard about GG's disgusting stage antics. We'd read all the reviews of his early records with The Jabbers in Maximum Rock'n'Roll. Somehow the newsprint of that mag looked faded even when it was new.

Although stories about GG entertained me, they had a more pronounced effect on Cheryl. She certainly surprised me last month after our candlelight dinner of roasted duck legs when she got all hot, bothered, and slinky, and asked me with cabernet-breath if I wanted to drink her piss like GG Allin. I took an enormous swig from my mug of whiskey and began hack-laughing as she stared right through me.

GG Allin's seething sense of hatred, as well as his willingness to embrace that he was a wreck, outlaw, and loser was refreshing to Cheryl, who'd been struggling as a science teacher at Woeselly Prep, her first job post-college. We'd also been casually trying to get her pregnant.

"He has a soft side. You don't believe me?" Cheryl had said some time later, nibbling at my earlobe as she rode me. She'd planted the first seed of my suspicion. As her grinding teeth glowed under the black light and her eyes rolled back, the growing distance I'd sensed between us had a logical explanation.

I pictured Cheryl pissing in GG Allin's face, then giving her soiled panties to him afterwards. According to my research of his other victims' accounts, he would rarely take off the panties entirely; instead, he'd cut out the front portion with a butterfly knife before allowing the golden shower to commence.

After this conversation, I began sleeping on the couch, whereas Cheryl wanted to see more and more of his shows in NYC. He'd been banned from most of the clubs in Boston for his feces- and blood-stained antics. She'd come home late, smelling of cigarettes and beer and wearing somebody else's studded, chalky leather jacket. Probably GG's, since its back featured a dead baby vampire painting beneath the phrase "Kill your children."

Yet Cheryl and GG's clandestine romance was ill timed and he was dead and gone before he and Cheryl knew that I knew. She'd gotten quite close with some of his hangers-on during her nights away from me in his gashed arms though, so we were invited to his funeral.

I managed to capture Jesus Christ Allin's tiny penis in a jar of formaldehyde during the event. After the party ended beside his open casket, I'd clipped it off with some pruning sheers from the maintenance man's tool shed beside the garden of St. Rose Cemetery.

I placed the jar on the kitchen table beneath the midnight moon, giddy with ideas for the little fellar's continued mutilation. The base of GG's severed penis sprouted sharp teeth where it had been severed from his body. It swirled around in the smudged jar, causing sparkling bubbles to rise and pop until it shook violently.

The ghosts of several sparrows and a giraffe stood beside the shaking jar as the penis's mouth laughed and cackled.

"What did you do to Cheryl, you piece of shock rocker shit? You had no talent. You just wanted to offend and annoy," I said.

"You have it all wrong. It was never my intention to shock. In fact, even having only a few followers in the early years assured me that I was not completely crazy or depraved, at least not beyond reach. I would have been a much more shocking and horrible person if I'd buried my true nature and pretended I was someone I wasn't," GG Allin's severed penis said.

Cheryl emerged from the bedroom, smelling of urine. I

hadn't seen her all week, other than at the funeral. She didn't even bother to acknowledge me. She sat down across from GG's talking penis, opened the jar, and set the piece of undead flesh in front of her.

She fellated the wormy blue phallus vigorously, but it failed to engorge and drooped whenever she released it from her lips.

"Oh yeah, Cheryl honey that feels great. Hope the embalming fluid isn't too rancid," GG's severed penis said.

She continued for a few hours, despite no tangible sign of arousal.

Eventually, Cheryl collapsed from nausea and exhaustion.

"Now that I have demonstrated my powers, you must return me to my master," GG Allin's severed penis said to me as Cheryl's prostrate body gurgled and belched. A ceramic figurine-sized hand swam from behind the penis' back and threw something at my face: a miniature GG sculpted from walnut-brown feces.

"You better listen," the tiny sculpture said as it crawled over my nose, stomping mushy footprints into my forehead and throwing tick-sized GG shit sculptures directly into my eyes, causing itchiness, red blotches, and a throbbing allergic reaction as my world was enveloped in darkness.

☠☠☠

A band of dirty punks screamed and blared their out-of-tune, electrified instruments above GG's grave while wearing jockstraps and skeleton masks, taking enemas, and throwing turds at each other.

A bass player slammed his forehead against the gravestone, then fell backwards unconscious as blood trickled down his forehead. The loss of the bass player hardly altered the band's sound, which was equivalent to a shoddy Scumfucs recording on scratched 90-gram vinyl.

A reddish light seeped through the cracked gravestone. Gelatinous, primordial, fetus-like blue and green fingers pulled apart the gravestone and GG emerged, albeit in an altered form: silky wings made of veined human skin drooped down his feminine back with the elegance of a mink shawl while 12-inch high heels that grew out of his feet elevated his already imposing frame.

Although he remained unmistakably GG, he had a perfectly formed vagina where his severed penis used to be. The cruddy "Fuck You" with the disproportionate middle finger tattooed on his left shoulder and the "Live Fast Die" motto above his left nipple remained.

As he began to perform, he exploded out of himself in a blurring animalistic rage. The songs were unexceptional three chord rock but sung with a demonic conviction and dirty energy, giving insight into a distorted worldview in songs like "Bite It, You Scum" and "I Wanna Fuck Myself."

Mesmerized, I swayed back and forth at the foot of GG's grave, feeling lighter and on the verge of tears.

I knew angels and wolves of the wind.

Cheryl crawled out of GG's grave wearing sparkling silver shards stitched together, but not covering her blonde-haired pussy or pink bubblegum nipples, just surrounding and accentuating them.

"You could've been an animal just like me and GG, if only you'd embraced your true and violent nature, just as it exists within us all," Cheryl said, her fiery snake tongue extending like a whip that singed my arm hairs and left a devil-goat brand on my shoulder blade.

"He was a vile, violent wolf who should've been shot dead. Sure, he understood his primal passions, but he exploited them, molesting and betraying so many women," I said.

GG extended his wings and began flipping over and over as three bright streams of purple, pink, and green piss issued from three different openings within the dips, crevices, bulbs, walls, and glistening dripping valleys of his elaborate vagina.

The band, as if in worship, played a sludgy version of "Bite It, You Scum," which made GG's butt wiggle as he floated with his multicolored piss soaring in three arcs. Although his genitals had changed, his body remained pudgy and bear-like, the same cruddy homemade tattoos prominent, although his skin now a much healthier and more resilient hue and sparkling lightly as if dusted by the silvery filaments of an alien plant.

"I never loved Cheryl. I only loved myself. And I never would've killed myself onstage or put her in danger if it wasn't for all the people chasing me through the Lower East Side streets after my final show. I lay down in front of a truck. I needed to collapse just then but everyone chased me into the street as I looked for the St. Mark's Hotel. I just wanted to disappear. Not perform right then. The audience was this monster I'd created. A demonic energy resulting from all that I'd thrown—tears, feces, dignity. My demonic offspring had come to haunt me and, even as my so-called friends took photographs with my corpse, I'd created a legion of my own hatreds, fanning for my attention, horny for my death wish," GG said.

☠☠☠

"It isn't supposed to be like this. It ain't supposed to be nothing like this," GG said.

I was with GG in his attic. My cheeks were painted with rouge and dotted eggshell freckles. My plaid dress was crisply ironed. A glowing green grasshopper escaped my mouth and floated, pulsing toy dragon fluorescents, until it landed in the rafters. GG smiled.

GG hunched over his sewing machine, affixing patches of "Scumfucs" and "GG" and "I Hate You" and "Die Parasites" onto a panther-black leather jacket.

I gazed at GG's armpit hairs. Within them, like a cooking stew, a swarm of soggy rats swirled round and round.

A slapping sound brought me back from my drowned rat

reverie: GG's intricate vagina was mere inches from my face and stank of rotten clams.

"Where is it?" he asked, obviously referring to his missing penis.

If I were not bound by rope, I may have laughed. GG's severed penis was in the chest pocket of my overall-like corduroy dress with a cherry-sized gag in its mouth and tightly tied up in shoelaces (I must have done it in a fugue) so mummy-like that even the most desperate struggle of its wormlike body would fail to alert GG of its presence.

"Do you want me to get out the fucking blowtorch?"

GG's intricate vagina unfolded into wide butterfly wings as a dragon-like tail unraveled. As his vulva detached itself, a coconut crab of inner labial flesh emerged and crawled towards me. Its cactus-textured tongue assaulted and enveloped my face. It was like being stuck in a compromised position beside an overly jolly dog. GG laughed and threw a Nerf football-shaped turd, hitting a direct bull's-eye in the center of my forehead.

This change in events only excited the coconut crab of labial flesh. It promptly gobbled the dripping log as if it contained delicious corn on a cob. Its skin immediately turned greenish and the entire attic revolved carousel-style. The attic spun faster and faster as the coconut crab made of labial flesh trotted and sauntered, as if to mock the cantering of a horse.

As GG and I were suctioned to the walls, the coconut crab made of labial flesh remained unaffected, trotting now in its former spot, although its skin color changed to new-toy ladybug red at first and then, as its movements grew slow and sickly, to the pallor of a Destroying Angel mushroom. Fangs dripped from its lips as its face shifted upwards in a spiraling rainbow swirl.

GG crawled towards me, sweating, pale, and nauseous. The pressure of the spinning room had evidently afforded his missing member the ability to loosen its bounds and wiggle out of the front pocket of my overall dress. It yawned its fanged worm mouth and looked enviously at the portal in GG's armpit where the dead rats swirled.

"Come to mother. Yes, child," GG said as his severed penis dove into the portal of his swirling armpit hairs and dead rats.

"Yes. You have him now. Just leave Cheryl alone," I said.

"Cheryl, baby," GG said, sticking his hand up his rectum.

And then I saw her trotting, trotting, trotting on a donkey made of shit in the palm of his hand.

I finally believed in happy endings, in the joy of enemas, and in my own reflected girlish glory in the eyes of one beholden girl.

THE FINAL FLIGHT OF THE CHRYSANTHEMUM BYZANTIUM

Nicholas Day

"One of the beginnings of human emancipation is the ability to laugh at authority." -Christopher Hitchens

In the year 2666, GG Allin was supposed to save us all. He sat at the controls to the massive starship, which the scientists named the Chrysanthemum Byzantium. It was a name GG hated. He hated its pretension. He hated its nostalgic connotations. He hated his role as a savior, when all he wanted to be was a prophet. He renamed the ship Carnival of Excess. It was a personal favorite of his albums, a tribute to Hank Williams, fellow outlaw.

"Computer," barked GG. "Play 'Carmelita.' I want it loud."

An electric voice, "As you wish, Mr. Allin," echoed through the hull.

He rocketed toward the last space station still functioning in Earth's orbit. There was a payload to be delivered, and GG was the only man to do it. Nobody else had the endurance to finish what they set out to fucking do. GG was the only one throwing monkey wrenches into the gears. After Iggy let him down, after Sid fell in love, then the Ramones praised shit like Guns 'N' Roses, when his brother and bandmates eventually died, and the rest of humanity went tits up, making garbage like Justin Bieber popular. And the K-pop invasion. Fuck. There were no allies, only boring assholes who embraced comfort and conformity. GG truly felt like an alien to the world.

Regardless, it was time for him to save mankind. Time to fight. Time for revenge.

Back in 2015, John Wayne Gacy descended from Heaven, an angel whose wings were made of feathers given as gifts from those he murdered in life, because all was forgiven in God's Kingdom. It was the first rule: absolve those who sin against you. Letting go of grudges, accepting God's Will, that's all you had to do. Otherwise, no admittance. It was an easy choice for most. In fact, almost everyone who was thought of as bad, all the notorious sinners, murderers, pederasts, junkies, despots, dealers . . . they were all with Him. Very few souls were in the boundless depths of Hell.

Gacy couldn't understand why his friend GG Allin ended up in Hell. Angels like Gacy weren't allowed to confer with the damned, nor allowed to set foot in Hell. But Gacy could find a way. He hatched a plan to save GG.

Getting a body was easy. Angels called it "soul-jacking," taking the ethereal form and enveloping the corporeal one. The ethereal is much stronger than the aura of a corporeal, and when the former encases the latter, one literally chokes out the other. It's like putting a mouse in a Ziploc bag. And Gacy quickly found his mouse.

Mr. Tully was a nebbish elderly man, a tax attorney, love-lorn. He wandered New York City streets, wishing he was young enough to paint the town red. Advanced age made sure it would only ever be a dream, a late regret. He gazed at his old apartment building on Central Park West. It was remodeled, hardly recognizable as the building he once lived in. His final thought was of the girl that got away. John Wayne Gacy set upon Tully, sealing him up and choking out his soul, sending him to Heaven.

Now to summon the Deadly Mothers, a trio of undead bad-asses, death cheaters, unwanted by Heaven or Hell. They could go where they wanted, when they wanted. They worked together, but worked for no one. They beat the system, and by doing so, they became a system of their own. The Deadly

Mothers could get you what you wanted, for a price. Harry Houdini was the leader de facto. His grave was in the city.

Machpelah Cemetery was rundown. The main office was abandoned decades ago. Growth overtook many of the smaller stones, but the Houdini grave was tended to, benefits of being a beloved legend. Summoning the magician was easy, if you knew what you were doing.

At the head of the plot was a large, decorative granite bench carrying the family name, Weiss, and the name of its most famous member, Houdini. At the center, just above the names, was an emblem of the Society of American Magicians. Above that, a bust of Harry. The bust was the key to calling Houdini forth, and it was instrumental to his escaping the clutches of Heaven and Hell. Graven images in a Jewish cemetery were sacrilegious. He was never allowed admittance to the beyond, never given a chance to offer absolution to those he judged in life. Since Hell could only take those who denied acceptance to Heaven, his soul was forced to wander.

Gacy wrenched the bust free from its perch, smashing it to pieces on the granite bench. Then he sat down to wait for an answer. He daydreamed of young men, drifted to sleep, courting an erection.

💀💀💀

"Why'd you call me?"

Gacy startled awake. Houdini stood before him, smoking a cigarette.

"I've heard you only smoke when you're nervous," Gacy said.

"Wouldn't you be nervous if your grave was vandalized by every charlatan and shit heel in the five boroughs?"

"I have a buddy that's stuck in Hell. Can you get him out?"

Houdini laughed. "Can I get him out, he says." Houdini smacked Gacy on the shoulder. "You're a laugh riot, pal. This is Harry Houdini you're talking to. I could sneak the Devil out of Hell."

"That's. . . that's great!"

"So, what's your name, buster? Who am I working for?"

"My name is John Wayne Gacy."

"Christ. You don't look like a fat clown."

"I borrowed this, um, body."

"Soul-jacker, eh? So, this poor schmuck died so you could bust your buddy out of Hell? Nice. They'll let a real piece of work like you into Heaven but I gotta roam. Unbelievable. Well, what's in it for me, huh? What's in it for ol' Harry?"

"What about the other Deadly Mothers?"

"C'mon, you're asking me to snatch one soul out of Hell. I don't need two other guys gumming up the works."

"But I rather wanted to meet Tesla and Maimonides."

"Well, tough rocks. You got me and that's all you're getting. Now what are you paying?"

"I. . . I don't know. Name your price, I suppose."

"Yeah, right." Harry took a long drag off his cigarette. "Tell you what. My wife, Bess, bless her heart, she's buried with the Catholics in Gate of Heaven Cemetery, up in Hawthorne. It's about an hour north of here. I want you to go get her. I want her buried next to me. You used to run a little cemetery under your house, right? This ought to be cake for you."

Gacy kicked aimlessly at the ground and wouldn't look up at Houdini.

"You get my wife and I'll get your buddy." Harry clapped his hands. "Does that sound like a good goddamn deal or what?"

They shook hands, worked out the finer details. Then they parted ways. Houdini, apparently, knew of an easy way to get to Hell. He gave Gacy a car key and a slip of paper with an address for a parking garage, so he'd have something to cart around the body. A couple nights later and Bess was the only Catholic buried in Machpelah Cemetery.

They decided to meet at 194 E 2nd St in the East Village.

That's where The Gas Station used to be, the last venue GG played before he died. But The Gas Station had been torn down, replaced with a Duane Reade, a 24-hour pharmacy. They could meet at night, which was good, because even though GG had been gone a long time, his legend hung around the place like a heavy musk.

Gacy wandered up and down the aisles, pretending to shop, when he heard a familiar voice.

"Where is the fucking Gas Station? What the fuck is this shit?" GG Allin stood in the aisle, Houdini trailing just a bit behind. GG wore his leather jacket, what looked like a new pair of jeans. In his right hand was a bottle of Jim Beam. In his left hand, a silver microphone. "I need a fucking guitar. Where the fuck is the rock 'n' roll in this place? Who the fuck are you, you fucking conformist?"

Gacy forgot that he wasn't quite himself, and that to his friend, Gacy looked like the elderly Mr. Tully. "It's me. It's Gacy."

"John Wayne Gacy?" GG looked back to Houdini, who only nodded back toward Gacy. "Why did you take me out of Hell?"

"I wanted to save you, GG. Everyone is in Heaven. It's great. It's so easy to get in."

"Fuck everyone. Fuck Heaven. Fuck you." He turned and pointed to Houdini. "And fuck this dude. I came here to play my rock 'n' roll, not go to some conformist shithouse, some crutch for the cripples. Do you know what I heard on the radio tonight? Bullshit! That's what. Lame corporate shit. Ass-kissers. Sell-outs. The radio is infected with that scene. Worst fucking music I ever heard. Where's the rock, goddammit? Where's the poison? I've been gone twenty-something years and this is what happened. You've all turned into safe, stupid, boring pussies. I said I need a guitar."

"But I saved you, GG. You can come be in Heaven, where you belong."

Houdini stepped past GG and held up a hand. "Yeah,

about that, the whole going back to Heaven bit. Look, when you take a soul out of Hell, Satan has a rule about that. You gotta give one in return. And you were so selfless about saving your, um, friend. I told Satan that he could have yours."

"My what?"

"Your soul, pal."

"But I did what you asked."

Houdini held his hands up. "I know, I know. Look, you wanted him out of Hell. You got what you wanted. And yes, you did me a big favor, too. But you have to pay the piper."

The front entrance to the Duane Reade exploded as two hulking, red demons crashed through it. The girl at the counter screamed, took a deep breath, and then screamed some more. The ten-foot-tall monstrosities clambered over each other in a fury, knocking over displays and gondolas with their tales and horns.

One of the brutes swept aside an entire shelf, exposing the terrified Gacy. The demons looked at each other and laughed, giving one another a high-five. One demon ripped the flesh from its chest. Its rib cage was hollow, like a tiny empty prison cell. The other demon snatched up Gacy, pulling off his arms and legs and head, swallowing each chunk in one gulp. It bent over and spread its ass cheeks, while the other demon lay on its back and opened its mouth, a willing toilet. The demon passed a steaming mess into the other's maw, and the demon stood up, carefully chewing and swallowing.

GG and Houdini watched every wet chunk fall into the exposed torso of the beast. The excrement didn't digest, but came together, rebuilding Gacy, a human-shit hybrid. "Jesus Christ, help me!" he screamed. The demons laughed again. The floor of the Duane Reade opened like a sinkhole, a fiery pit that must've been a one-way ticket to Hell. The demons jumped in. The hole closed. GG and Houdini looked at each other.

"I need a guitar."

"Not a problem."

☗☗☗

GG Allin got his guitar. Houdini saw to that. With no other business or interest between the two, they parted ways. Houdini appreciated GG's disregard for authority. GG felt an affinity for a man who could piss off God enough to get permanently kicked out of the afterlife. They shook hands, saying nothing, walking away in opposite directions. Houdini went back to his grave in Queens. GG was drawn to the setting sun, the west.

He soon found his brother, Merle. In an interview years later, Merle would be asked if he had been surprised to see his brother return from the grave. "GG was crazier than the Devil. I'm not surprised he got kicked out of Hell."

Right away, GG confided in his brother the plan for their comeback show. "We're going to have a concert on Hank Williams' grave." GG sipped his bourbon. "You got to invite mom, but don't let her know I'm back. I want it to be a surprise."

"Holy shit, GG." Merle shook his head. "The Murder Junkies are getting back together."

"No!" GG yelled. "No, they're not. It's not the Murder Junkies anymore. It's the Rock 'N' Roll Underground. Murder Junkies became a scene, and I ain't doing that shit. This is new shit. New allies. No poser fucks. Somebody shows up in a Murder Junkies t-shirt, they get the shit kicked out of them. I have such a fierce, intense fire burning inside of me that just wants to explode. I am the true underground messiah. You come to my show, you're going to a war. And I'm out for violence, chaos, lawlessness, all the way. I don't care about anybody or anything, except for myself and my mission."

The brothers swapped bourbon until they fell asleep. Merle jarred awake just before dawn, when everything outside was glowing blue, like the world was a ghost. GG stood in front of him, naked. He'd pissed on the carpet and on the couch. It smelled like alcohol.

"I can't do the shit thing anymore. I can't shit on stage."

"Well, fuck, man, everybody goes through a phase. I don't think anybody is gonna be too sad if you don't smear shit everywhere."

"Fuck, Merle, it was never a fucking phase. It's not like when we were kids, jerking each other off. I mean, I literally can't shit. Ever. I made a promise."

"What kind of crazy motherfucker promises to never shit ever again? You'll explode."

"No, brother, I won't. And I made that promise to somebody important."

"Jesus, some fucking girl?"

"No. Satan. The Devil himself. He made me promise."

"You pissed all over the floor, you fucking drunk."

GG squatted down in front of Merle, putting a hand on his brother's knee. "You know, man, there aren't a whole lot of people in Hell." GG tipped back and sat on the piss-soaked carpet. He folded his legs beneath him and gently rocked, squishing and sloshing in his own urine. "One of the only people I could talk to was this fucking dude named Oscar Wilde. You know him?"

"He used to write plays 'n' shit."

"You know what he said to me? He said 'The best thing about being here is that we're not supposed to be here,' and by here he meant Hell. He said authority was degrading, that it turns us into conformists, turns us into pets, like a dog or a cat or some shit. He said we think other people's thoughts, live by other people's standards, wear other people's second-hand clothes. He said people never be themselves for a single moment. And that was why we were in Hell. He said we were like brothers, me and him. I asked him if he thought he was a scumfuc outlaw and he laughed and smacked his knee and yelled 'Yes' at the top of his lungs. He never let me call him Oscar or Mr. Wilde after that. He only wanted to be called Scumfuc."

"Cool dude."

"Yeah, man, a real ally in the trenches, right? So, here comes this guy named Harry Houdini, and him and Satan are fucking yelling and screaming at each other like a fucking husband and wife. And they're carrying on like that about me. And Harry, he says something about Satan not having dominion over him and to fuck off, that he's taking me out of Hell and ain't shit the Devil can do.

"But ol' Scratch says he does have dominion over me, so there's gotta be a deal, right? I gotta give something up. And that's when Scumfuc asks me if I ever read his book. Fuck no, I say. But Harry knows it and Satan knows it. Something about a portrait that eats all this dude's sin and keeps him living forever. And Scumfuc tells the Devil to let my shit fester in me forever, to keep me going as long as I never shit ever again. Satan laughed his ass off, laughed for way too long. And he said yeah, Scumfuc, that's the ticket, and the Devil stuck a finger up my butt and made me promise to never shit ever, and as long as I never shit again I could come back and live forever."

"Sounds good, man." Merle rolled to his side, away from the light creeping through the windows. "I got to sleep. We got a show tomorrow."

GG Allin and the Rock 'N' Roll Underground played over the grave of Hank Williams. News of GG's return hit Twitter, then Facebook, then the local news came out. National news picked up the story. Oakwood Annex Cemetery in Montgomery, Alabama was filled with folks coming to see the risen Christ. GG leapt into the crowd, punching and kicking, made people touch his cock. There were screams. There were cheers. There were cops, arresting everybody in sight. The town hadn't seen that much action since the bus boycotts.

GG was the number one news story. Zombie, they called him. Miracle. He told his tale to anyone who would listen. ABC, CBS, NBC, CNN, they all wanted GG Allin. He told them he was immortal, that he was God. A journalist for Rolling Stone asked him about the return of "poop punk." GG smacked the journo across the mouth.

"When I wake up tomorrow, I'll still look the same way,

I'll still smell the same way." He pointed to his butt. "*This* is not a show. *This* is not an act." GG kicked his chair away and got up on top of the journalist's desk. "*I* am the guy. *I* am the king. I rule the Rock 'N' Roll Underground. I'm bringing revolution against the government. Against the police. Against any form of society that is trying to put us down and restrict us in any way.

"My pal Scumfuc said you cannot conform. You must be a true non-conformist. To hell with what your parents say. I am the man. All you have to do is listen to what I have to say. I want it all and I'm gonna have it all, because I am everything." GG lifted up a sleeve, brandishing old and new scars. "I self-mutilate. I beat the shit out of my audience. If they're in my way I take them out. I don't care. There is no poop punk. I'm not shitting on stage for anyone or anything. You come to *my show*, you don't get what *you* want. You get what you *deserve*. You can challenge me. I have no problem with that. I like the confrontation, but you're gonna lose."

Allin was even invited onto The View. Whoopi Goldberg asked him, "Are there any special ladies out there for GG? What would you want them to know about you?"

GG snorted. He leaned back into his chair, kicking one of his dirty boots onto the table. "We're infected with AIDS. We fuck every day, and we kill everything we fuck. So, whadya think about that?"

The interview only lasted the one question. He was escorted out by police when he punched Nicolle Wallace in the face. Los Angeles court sentenced him to nine months in prison for aggravated assault. He penned a single letter while serving his time. It was copied and sent to Pope Francis, Rabbi David Lau, Rabbi Yitzhak Yosef, and Khalifatul Masih V. It read:

Dear Phonies,

Your children, if you got children out there, they're going to be my children. My flock. I'm going to own those kids. I'm going to own their souls. They're going to do anything that I say, because I'm the King, and they can identify with Me, because the real, true nonconformist children in this country are sick and tired of their parents, their schools, the people force-feeding them what to do. I am the answer. When they listen to My lyrics and they listen to My songs, they're listening to the way it really should be. You know that, and I know that. Your kids are my kids.

Yours in Hell,
Jesus Christ Allin

GG and Merle's mother, Arleta, passed away before his release. Unable to attend her funeral, GG became sullen, distraught. He was given an early release due to the circumstances, and with a hope that the trauma may have woken up the civilized man buried inside the layers of animal instinct.

He dug up Arleta's remains. He sat with her and played "Carmelita" on the guitar given to him by Houdini. Merle answered a call from the local precinct. It was a federal offense. GG was charged to the fullest, three years in a state prison, complete with psych evaluation and 24/7 monitoring.

"Are you a happy person?" asked the psychiatrist.

"I'm beautiful," was GG's only reply.

He would not have an early release.

☠☠☠

An influenza epidemic in the fall of 2020 wiped out hundreds of millions of people across the globe. Even GG got sick, but he didn't die. Merle wasn't as lucky. The brothers held hands, their hospital beds pushed up next to each other, intravenous fluids dripping into their bodies.

Merle tugged on GG's hand, but his brother was unresponsive. Heavy sedation made it hard for GG to stay awake. Merle knew what was coming, he whispered to his sleeping brother, "Touring with you was the greatest experience of my life. I never got on stage and did the same thing night after night, like most of those lame-ass boring bands. I saw something different, something new, and something exciting. Every night." Merle died with a smile on his face. GG woke up, and then knew what Merle must have felt on the morning of June 28, 1993.

"I'm going to save you," GG said. "I'm going to save all of you."

💀💀💀

CCTVs caught footage of GG Allin sneaking into Mexico circa 2100. Two years later, South African students in Johannesburg blogged about seeing Allin play a live set, wearing the eviscerated body of a shark like a pair of overalls. He'd asked them to pledge allegiance to him and to the Rock 'N' Roll Underground.

A handful of journalists investigated these incidents, tracking dozens of similar stories, unannounced concerts, costumes made from dead animals, requests of allegiance, and young people that were all too eager to pledge.

Some people wondered if GG was forming a cult. Others speculated that GG died decades ago, that whoever was performing these concerts had taken the moniker and was impersonating him. And everyone made sure to mention the lack of shitting on stage, even though Allin hadn't done that since before his death was staged in the late 20th century.

Stories about these shows became less frequent. The last concert was blogged about late in 2124. It was said to have taken place near the pyramids of Giza. GG was noted to have been dressed in the carcass of a camel, screaming lyrics, thrashing a guitar. The crowd gathered before him was numbered in the hundreds.

Then, GG disappeared, again.

💀💀💀

GG Allin reappeared in the United States in early 2600. It was a media circus. Three different doctors confirmed through DNA tests that he was, in fact, the real deal. Pundits dubbed him the Impossible Man. Asked where he had been, Allin told tales of being accepted into the Jewish faith while living in seclusion in Israel, even having become a rabbi. He spent later years with the Pakistani peoples, embracing Islam, claiming to have become accepted as a mullah. He claimed to have missed his home and wanted to return, to give something positive back to the country that birthed him. He promised to share the secrets of his immortality.

Then, in 2666, the last great war broke out. It was not among governments or people of differing faiths, one economy against another. It was a war between humanity and an alien being that called itself God.

First, God descended upon the world. He brought with him an army of winged humanoids. They slaughtered countless beings in that first week. Humans, animals, nothing living was safe.

After that, God used his arcane technology to raise the dead. Cemeteries erupted like swelling pustules across the skin of our planet. Reanimated corpses swarmed city streets.

A military operation was organized with the joint efforts of any nation willing to participate. The entire world fought against God. Allin worked his way quickly up the ranks, eventually commanding a division of human and robot soldiers.

General Allin rallied his troops at the Battle of Austin. "When you have the power to fight, you fight. When you lose the power, you kill yourself or I'll kill you." It was a massive victory, and a turning point in the war. Allin was hailed a hero, not just in the United States. Everyone across the planet felt indebted to him. He was seen as the first true global leader, strong, yet diffident.

When God and his armies retreated to the skies, a great swathe of the population went with him, either killed in an attack or by roving bands of the undead, leaving pockets of survivors. The human race was seriously courting extinction. Scientists turned to the Impossible Man for help.

"Let us study you, GG," they begged. "We can take you to the Space Station Sagan. We have people there that can unlock the secrets to your immortality. You may be the key to saving our race."

GG laughed. "What if I told you it's because I can never take a shit, that my own death is lost somewhere up my asshole? What then?"

The scientists, in their desperation, collectively shrugged their shoulders. "Does it even matter?"

💀💀💀

GG addressed the entire world in a global telecast. He told the people that he was leaving Earth. Saving the human race was his scene now. He asked only one thing in return.

"Give your allegiance to me. Accept me as your leader. Your savior." And the world embraced him as such.

"Erect a statue of me in the Mount of Olives, and another in the Wadi Al-Salaam." And the people of the world did as they were told.

💀💀💀

The night before launch, GG was visited by the reanimated corpse of John Wayne Gacy. He was completely desiccated, mostly rotting bones. He couldn't speak, though he carried a pen and pad of paper. He wrote on it, in all caps.

YOU ABANDONED ME

I WAS IN HELL

GG nodded his head. He embraced his rotting friend, held his skull with both hands, like a lover might, and told him, "You thought you were saving me, when I was saving you all along. I'm telling you, my friend, that I created myself inside the womb from the fires of Hell. There are no separations between Jesus Christ, God and the Devil, because I am all of them. I am here to take Rock 'N' Roll back and prove to the world that I am the real king, through the powers I have acquired. When I was born in 1956, Rock 'N' Roll first started taking off. Why do you think that was? Because I created it. I created Elvis. I saved you. I made it all happen. Even before I was born I was plotting. Trust me. Do you trust me?"

Gacy scribbled on his pad.

YES I DO

☻☻☻

The Chrysanthemum Byzantium, named for a scientist from Chicago and another from Istanbul, respectively, flew ever closer to Space Station Sagan. A phrase, Carnival of Excess, was written in blood across the main control deck. GG manned the controls. The other astronauts had died shortly after exiting earth's orbit, throttled by Allin.

"Computer," barked GG. "Play 'Carmelita.' I want it loud."

The ship's A.I. buzzed, "Do you want to switch to auto-pilot?"

"No." GG laughed. He guzzled the liquid laxative he'd smuggled onboard. His guts were churning while Chrysanthemum Byzantium rocketed toward inevitability.

Scientists aboard Space Station Sagan had expected to receive GG in order to study him, to unlock the secrets of his life, and in doing so they hoped to use those secrets to save the peoples of Earth. But GG had his own plans. Death, he reckoned, was its own salvation.

When the Chrysanthemum Byzantium made impact with Space Station Sagan, Allin filled the legs of his space suit with 666 years of shit, and then there was an explosion that could be seen from Earth. People marveled at what they thought was a meteor shower, not realizing it was GG's shit burning up upon re-entry.

☠☠☠

Because of the graven images erected in the Jewish and Islamic cemeteries, GG wasn't allowed into Heaven, neither could he enter Hell. Because of his final bowel movement, his contract with Satan was null and void. He was in debt to no one, and walked the earth, like Houdini, a phantasmagorical thing. However, because the peoples of the earth had given their allegiance to Allin, shunning God in the process, he slowly amassed an army of souls that were likewise denied a traditional afterlife.

"You and your children, they're my children. My flock. I own you. I own your souls. I'm the King. And this is the Rock 'N' Roll Underground."

☠☠☠

And GG Allin lorded over the lost souls of earth until its final days, until the heat death of the universe, in a new Heaven of his making, and he was God, because fuck you.

AP-3498

Richard Arnold

John.

John.

John Atkins. The name crawled to the front of his mind as he slowly opened his eyes, his vision gradually clarifying through the smoke and steadily-blinking lights.

Captain John Wesley Atkins lay strapped into his command chair in the center of the cockpit. He moved his head to look around and take stock of the situation. Red alarm strobes pulsed gently through the haze, and electric sparks burst periodically out of smashed instrument panels and severed power cables. The events of the last few minutes creeped back into his memory, joining together like pieces of a puzzle.

Suicide mission, Atkins thought, grinning mildly. *Nearly successful.*

Atkins looked over at the seat to his right, studying the motionless form of Ronald Logan, Chief Science Officer. "Logan," he whispered hoarsely.

As he leaned over to touch him, to rouse him from unconsciousness, an explosion of pain shot through his body. He rebounded back as he let out a startled scream through clenched teeth. His focus darted to his limp left arm. *Broken,* he thought.

Steadying himself as the pain faded, Atkins used his right arm to carefully remove the restraining buckles securing him to the chair. He braced himself to lift the v-shaped torso restraints over his head, then slumped back in the chair and drew a deep breath. He looked down at the floor grating beneath his feet, then maneuvered off the chair, gradually standing upright with a woozy uncertainty.

The cockpit of the N.S.S. Wanderer was in ruins. Supply

containers and footlockers lay thoroughly smashed, their contents spread liberally around the area. Tiny shards of the now-shattered navigation globe covered every surface. Communication and power cabling dangled from junction boxes and ceiling panels, the viscera of a dead ship, now exposed for all to see.

Atkins approached Officer Logan, then stopped and merely stared. The intermittent emergency lights above Logan's chair illuminated the scientist's head, smashed open by a shattered overhead support beam, the bulk of which now lay in his lap, saturated in an expanding puddle of blood and brain.

Never did like wearing the helmet, Atkins thought, a brief moment of dark satisfaction quickly vanishing before a rising tide of panic.

Atkins thought back to the days of training for the mission. Working alongside Logan, encouraging his progress, reassuring the terrified scientist the night before the launch, as they both stood behind the launch pad's security fence, staring up at the massive rocket. He remembered how Logan had clutched the chain-link, quietly stammering his wish to be left behind, for the mission to be scrubbed, for the revelation that this had all been some elaborate practical joke. The scientist's body now sat for Atkins' quiet inspection. The terrified grimace on the young man's face had been at once locked in place and put to rest by the shaft of steel that killed him.

After several long seconds, he gathered himself and began checking the cockpit to take stock of what equipment remained usable. At the main control console, he flipped switches at random until one of the screens glowed: Atmospherics. A few additional attempts to activate the other stations were fruitless. *Totally blind to everything except what's in the air*, he thought. *Perfect.*

He reviewed the current readout: it told the tale of what N.S.S. scientists had theorized all along: the little brown planet had no atmosphere. *A dead, lifeless rock*, he thought.

He went for the ULF radio transmitter, but then caught

himself short. He stared at the handset for a moment, then drew a deep breath and turned back around. *Not like they're sending an ambulance my way anytime soon.*

Atkins carefully maneuvered around the wreckage scattered on the floor, collecting anything that seemed intact. But after twenty minutes of searching and an additional hour of minor repair-work, he had at his disposal only a portable grav-meter, an emergency parachute, and a half-empty oxygen tank for his spacesuit.

The wavering indicator on the grav-meter read just around 1 Earth gravity.

"Tell me something I don't know," he muttered to himself, and tossed the meter away in disgust.

He sat down and stared at the floor for several minutes as he thought through the details of his predicament. Finally he looked at the main exit hatch and sighed deeply. "If I'm already dead on this rock I may as well stretch my legs."

From the parachute, he crafted a makeshift sling for his broken arm. He then awkwardly strapped the oxygen tank to his back, nearly falling several times in the process. After checking his spacesuit's air seals and oxygen levels, he stepped in front of the hatch's access panel. One last time, he turned back to the wreckage of the cockpit, the flickering alarm lamps, Logan's corpse slumped in his chair. He then turned to the panel again, closed his eyes, and opened the hatch.

💀💀💀

The messages had arrived intermittently at first, faintly, but the signal strength had gradually increased over the years. They eventually began to reappear on a more regular basis, falling into a dependable cycle. The listening stations of the National Space Center had been recording the signals to wire recorder tape, the technicians cataloging them, interpreting them as best they could. What had first been noted in a late-night logbook entry as mere rhythmic chuffing over the drone of the background radiation of space was now understood to be something different. Organized. Intelligent. And not just structured, composed, but...something else. Something inexplicably, darkly human lay sequestered in those wavelengths.

The secretaries who caught the beginning of each signal's cycle blushed as they hurriedly transferred the line to the tape-recording technicians in the building next door. The officers at the N.S.C. with access to the tapes whispered the generalities of their secret reports to each other in the Space Center's hallways and parking garages. To each other, they admitted a discomfort with what they heard through the headphones, an ever-rising dread within them that they held at bay as best they could. A darkness pervaded the sounds, the audible tones mere carrier waves for something hidden, something larger: a huge, lurking, dread-soaked caterwauling from out of the Void.

Locating the source of the signals proved a massive undertaking, requiring the efforts of dozens of N.S.S. scientists, technicians, and more than a few anonymous tips from assorted ham radio enthusiasts. Finally, the listening station honed in on the source: a far-off exoplanet in a neighboring arm of the Milky Way, listed in the N.S.S. star charts as AP-3498. An otherwise unremarkable brown ball of rock circling a cool, yellow star light years away.

A massive, if hastily assembled, engineering project was put forward under great secrecy. It's goal: to build a rocket large and fast enough to carry a small crew to AP-3498 to investigate the origin of the signals and report back the findings.

It was here that Captain John Atkins entered the picture.

John Wesley Atkins had entered the National Space Service straight out of high school. Over seventeen years, he had proven himself a capable, if unremarkable, spaceman. Perpetually out of the public eye, and now middle-aged, twice-divorced, and childless, he fell under the crosshairs of N.S.S. Mission Command. Passed over for countless pioneering adventures in the past, he, now at the twilight of his career, suddenly found himself the perfect candidate for the greatest adventure Man had ever known. Mission Command's proposal was straightforward: he and a recently recruited, perpetually nervous radiotelegraphy specialist were to rocket to the exoplanet and investigate the signals.

He took a few days to think it over. In that time, he slept little and drank more than his usual share of Scotch. Eventually he signed on. Atkins knew well that this mission, conceived of and cloaked in secrecy, was a journey only a handful would ever know about. And the odds of returning safely home were slim at best. He was, of course, the perfect candidate to lead the mission: A functional but relatively insignificant part of the human race, a man without any real stake in the world's affairs.

Captain Atkins and the newly-promoted "Science Officer" Logan spent the better part of two years rocketing towards exoplanet AP-3498, running tests, cataloging stars, checking and re-checking instruments, fuel lines, telephone cabling. Bickering loudly, shouting each other down on occasion. Two men caught in an overheated steel tube headed straight for No-One-Knew-Where.

The small planetoid eventually came within sight, and during the mission's last few weeks gradually grew in size within their viewscope. The small relief they experienced when the rocket finally reached orbital distance of the planet was quickly extinguished when a fuel line ruptured and fire broke out in the main gravitational harness.

Crippled and pulled in by the planet's gravity well, there was nothing for the men to do. No adjustment maneuvers or g-braking would make any difference now. Cleared of all obstacles, each spaceman's ego opened like a pressure valve on the other. They screamed useless epithets at each other as they strapped in and braced themselves for the end to arrive. Fire licked the rocket's side viewports as the planet's flat brown surface rushed up at them.

A sudden jolt as the rocket hit atmosphere, and Atkins was knocked unconscious.

☠☠☠

Atkins stared out the opened hatch into the darkness. He paused to take in any available details, then pushed himself forward with his good arm. Grabbing hold of the upper edge of the hatch, he slowly lowered himself down to the uncertain ground, then stood up straight.

Everywhere stretching to the horizon was bathed in a deep dusk. Above him was a cloudless sky, revealing the blanket of stars providing what little light existed. A subtle flash of light appeared in the corner of his vision, and he turned in its direction. He stared for a moment and took in occasional flashes of what appeared to be red lightning, barely cracking through the darkness. Lingering on the sight, he noticed that the flashes centered on, and revealed, some kind of break in the uniform flatness of the horizon. Some subtle feature of the landscape, a mountain, a building, a ship...he couldn't be certain.

He turned around, trying to see any other feature at all. *Just a black empty slate*, he thought. He rested his hand on the hatch door, and peered back inside the broken hulk of the rocket. *No food. No water. No oxygen other than what's in the suit. Just waiting to die here,* he thought, closing his eyes and breathing deep. *Sit here in this rocket and rot, or roll the dice.* He took another breath, opened his eyes, and set out to walk into the unknown.

The flickering illumination of the distant lightning, and the subtle outlines of the structure it revealed, provided just enough of a landmark to navigate towards. He walked quickly, constantly checking the ticking clock that was his suit's oxygen gauge. *Fifty-two percent. An hour if I'm lucky.*

He looked around constantly, vigilant for signs of life, signs of shelter, of...anything. Fear crept over him, a primitive vulnerability tugging at his animal instincts. The darkness spawned countless shapes and figures in his vision, forms that vanished as quickly as they appeared. From time-to-time he touched his hand to the hip holster that once held his standard-issue Mark IV laser pistol. *Lost somewhere in that damned heap of a rocket*, he lamented.

He looked up at the stars, the alien constellations, the faint wisp of galactic spiral splitting the black in two, and at once took in the shocking insignificance of his presence here. Reduced from proud representative of Humanity to mere slow-moving prey, subject to the whims and predations of a dark alien world.

He returned his focus to the horizon, and to the structure, and continued his march.

Through the occasional flashes of what lay in the distance, the structure grew in his vision as he approached. Broad strokes of its outline slowly stacked in his brain. He trudged onward, one exhausted step after another, prodded on by the slow backwards movement of his oxygen gauge.

After what felt like days, he stopped finally before the structure and gazed up at it: a towering monolith, hundreds of feet tall. A massive, black spire, wrapped in thin, vine-like pathways. At the top sat a rounded pyramidal shape. If nothing else, it served as a lightning rod for the electrical storm that had guided him to this point. The sky overhead, absolutely blank everywhere else, was here coated in a swirling maelstrom of clouds, directing their fury at the tower that rose to meet them.

Atkins checked his oxygen gauge. *Three percent. Practically dead.*

He took a quick look around him and, still seeing nothing, began to jog towards the tower. He prayed for a door, a pressure chamber, a functioning radio. Something.

Reaching the structure, he felt along its smooth, black surface as he walked the perimeter. *Nothing. Not a goddamned thing!* His heart raced as he ran, faster and faster, the flicker of his oxygen alarm lamp glowing softly in the corner of his eye. His hand moved up and down the curved wall as he circled, grasping for detail, finding nothing but smooth blankness.

He was at a full run now, the sound of his breath roaring

154

in his ears. His lungs sucked at the hot carbon dioxide filling his suit. He circled the tower once, twice, began a third time around, searching for some detail he had missed before. Vision dimming, he staggered, gave out a sob, and collapsed to his knees in the alien dirt.

All options exhausted, he tensed every muscle in his body and screamed. A deep, aching bellow shaking the glass of his helmet. A cry at the end of the universe, going nowhere, reaching no one.

He fell suddenly to his side, the weight of his oxygen tank rolling him just as quickly onto his back. He looked up at the stars as his air-starved body began to spasm. The stars disappeared. A dark shape gradually blocked them out. A figure in silhouette drifted into Atkins' dimming vision,. An organic shape, a being. A human. A man. Unprotected from the ravages of this place, unsuited, entirely naked.

Atkins stared into the shapes that became the Man's dark eyes. His gaze drifted from the Man's hairless head, down to his ink-black beard and mouth, a grimace filled with stained, crooked teeth. An impossible thing on this lifeless planet. A stalker, a demon, a dark angel in this barren void.

The Man knelt and reached down behind Atkins' helmet, cradled his head, and leaned close to his face. Atkins' heart raced as his body shook and starved for air. Tears filled his eyes, fear overtaking him, but as he gazed in the Man's eyes, a feeling of calm came over him. Two strangers here at the end of the Universe, apart now from the human race, now truly alone.

The radio in Atkins' helmet gently crackled to life. The Man's mouth moved along with the words that came through. A rush of familiarity struck Atkins. The messages he had first heard so many years ago, the signals that had brought him here to this place, now played over his radio.

Exchanging your life
For my adventure

Atkins laid back, listened, and silently spoke along with the words he still remembered.

As calling cards creep into a tombstone

And a wave of tranquility shut his eyes and stilled his struggle.

And as sure as light scatters cockroaches
I, too, am gone

BONUS TRACKS

BORED WITH BRUTALITY

MP Johnson

Bored with everything, GG Allin decided to take a new approach to life.

He'd punched. He'd pooped. He'd bled. He'd fucked. He'd fucking rocked. He'd spent a decade outraging to the fullest extent possible, and now it just made him yawn. He couldn't even shoot heroin and shit in some whore's mouth while jerking off two faggots without falling asleep. To be fair, it was really good heroin.

When being brutal turned boring, he reasoned that the only non-boring thing he could possibly do, the only thing he hadn't ever really done before, was to try being normal for a change. He could just be a regular dude.

This wasn't going to be easy. He had stains from three separate vomits on his shirt. Driving his pinky finger into his belly button, he scraped out a wad of dried shit. Absentmindedly, he stuck his pinky into his mouth and sucked it clean while trying to remember the last time he had dropped a load. He would definitely need to shower. Yes, step one would be to take a shower and get clean clothes.

Technically though, he didn't have a home. Shoving aside the cardboard he had slept under, he looked around the alley. He didn't actually know where he was. His last gig had been in Chicago. A week ago? Two? He was probably still in Chicago. Where was the rest of the band? Fuck them. He didn't need them. If he was going to follow his plan, he couldn't turn to them for help.

They were all fucking nuts anyway. Merle? Dino? They may have had just enough normalcy to hold down places to live, but they were still nuts. Nuts, nuts, nuts. Boring and nuts. "Oh, let's go fuck a prostitute," GG mimicked out loud. "Let's do some coke." The words even tasted fucking boring on his tongue. Fuck the Murder Junkies and their boring, tedious debauchery. Fuck whores. Fuck drugs. He pulled a baggie of dope out of his jockstrap and tossed it in a dumpster. He was on the road to normal now, and it felt so wrong, so gloriously, wonderfully wrong.

He stepped out of the alley. He walked and walked, trying to figure out what he needed to do to fully commit to normality. Unfortunately, even with his heroin haze fading, he couldn't think of any way to complete the transition without engaging in one last boring criminal act. So he walked all the way to the suburbs, and he walked right up to a nice little house with light yellow siding. Not piss yellow, which the old GG would have loved, but a nice, sunny yellow that totally fit the bill for new, normal GG. He went around to the rear and busted open the back door with a surprisingly quiet and perfectly placed kick.

The back door led to the kitchen, where he peeled off his shirt and jockstrap and combat boots and tossed his only three articles of clothing into the garbage. There were three bins: recycling, organic and trash. He looked into the one labeled trash. It barely had anything in it, and what was there looked too clean. He was used to trashcans filled with dirty needles and whiskey bottles stuffed with cigarette butts. But he threw his refuse clothes in there nonetheless. Out with the old.

He found the shower and took a long, steamy soak. The hot water slowly penetrated the layers of shit and vomit and cum and blood. A snake shedding its skin. The detritus pooled in a brown soup around his feet.

Finished, he shaved off his scraggly facial hair. Without it, without the grime, even with the scars and tattoos, he looked surprisingly normal. Innocent. Perhaps even soft. He had never developed the hard lines that most men did, at least not on his face. He had put on some muscle in prison, so he did have some claim to masculinity. Not that he wanted it. He liked the intimidation that came with strength, but he despised the concept of the man's man.

He thought back to his high school days, when he wanted to be beautiful, when he wore his hair long and flowing, and he knew what to do with makeup. He'd get called a faggot, and he'd take it, even though he knew the label didn't quite fit. In recent years, he still let his inner femininity out whenever he could steal a miniskirt in his size or convince some cunt to paint his nails. Fewer people called him out on it these days.

He found the bedroom. A totally normal bedroom. Off-white walls. Nicely made bed. A shelf full of puppets. He picked up one of the puppets. A blue-skinned humanoid with a burlap eye patch.

Guess this is what normal people have in their pads, he thought, rather than sacks of fertilizer and old drum sets and passed out groupies.

He returned the puppet to the shelf and started digging through closets. He found the wife's clothes first. Dresses. He was tempted to try them on, but he needed to put that behind him. He was going to be a normal man. So he kept digging until he found normal men's clothes. Black slacks. Polo shirts. A perfect fit too. He looked in the mirror. A perfectly normal man in perfectly normal clothes.

But then the front door swung open.

He heard two voices. Two giggling voices. It was time for him to leave. Except he really liked this house, this not-piss-yellow house. He liked the clothes.

So he let the giggling couple find him. He knew he must have had the normal look down just right when, instead of screaming, the couple merely went quiet for a moment and said, "Oh hello, I think you're in the wrong house."

They did, however, scream as soon as GG came at them. He started with the man, delivering a perfect blow between the eyes that caused the man to drop to the floor. The success of the punch excited GG. Was this what fighting was like for normal, not-high people? Blows landing where intended, rather than spiraling out into the ether like defective fireworks? Normal people don't fight, he reminded himself. This is just one last dip into non-normality before he fully committed.

He kicked the woman between the legs and she fell to her knees. He grabbed a picture off the wall and gouged the corner of its heavy wooden frame into her skull, once, twice, three times until she stopped moving and he was sure she wouldn't move anymore. Blood splattered across the shelf full of puppets.

GG got down on hands and knees and sank his teeth into the man's throat. He tore out the adam's apple and chewed on for a minute. It was like putting an entire chicken wing in his mouth. He spit it out quick. This was not how normal people killed each other.

He ran to the bathroom and washed his face.

That night, he buried the couple in the backyard.

The next day, he proactively stopped at each neighbor's house and gave this spiel, using the name his mother had given him, the name he had abandoned so long ago: "Hi, I'm Kevin. I'm David Bannister's, your next-door neighbor's, brother. He and his wife Jill wanted me to stop by today because they didn't have enough time yesterday. They signed on for a five year mission to help in Nepal, rebuilding after the earthquake, and I'm going to be staying in their home while they're over there. If you need anything, let me know. I want to be a good neighbor!"

Each time he delivered the spiel, the voice in his head that said "I bet her cunt tastes like salted deli meat" or "I'd like to lick his scrotum clean" got fainter and fainter. GG Allin's voice got fainter and fainter.

Eventually, Kevin could hardly hear it.

Within a month, he had a job. He had assumed David Bannister's identity for work purposes, which came with a business degree and a pretty solid resume, so he didn't have trouble landing a six figure salary as manager of customer operations of the local branch of a multinational tech corporation. It was very normal. Most of his work entailed sending emails telling people to check with other people to find out what to tell different people to do in order to get something done. It was easy.

There was one situation. One day, one of his underlings came into his office and made a blanket statement about how Kevin AKA David didn't spend enough time coaching his team and helping them be the best they could be. Kevin shattered his coffee mug on the desk and pressed a shard of ceramic against the employee's neck, hard enough to draw blood.

"Be the best you can be or I will peel off your face and use it as a cum rag," Kevin coached.

The employee ran out crying. Thankfully, Kevin had been doing such a good job of being normal, he convinced the board of directors that the confrontation hadn't happened and the employee was trying to frame him. They fired the employee.

Kevin got a nice, normal routine together. A morning run. A stop at the coffee shop. Work. An evening of books and television programs.

During one of his regular pre-work coffee shop stops, he was standing in line when someone tapped him on the shoulder. He had fallen into a daydream about which of the various pastries he should choose: Danish? Donut? And the tap came perfectly timed to pull him out of the daydream just as it shifted into thoughts of shoving these pastries up his asshole.

"It's your turn to order," the voice said, not rude, not angry, almost soothing.

"Thank you," he said, without turning around.

He placed his order and went on his way. As he walked away from the coffee shop, he heard that voice again.

"Excuse me," the voice said.

He turned to see a woman. Early thirties. Light makeup. Glowing skin.

"I've seen you before," she said, with a sly smile.

Kevin's stomach sank. He thought of all the talk show appearances, preaching his vitriol, preaching his truth while clad in a military helmet. He should have known this would happen. He should have known he could not just be normal.

"Yeahhhhhh," he said, shrugging.

"You come here every day, don't you?"

The relief felt wonderful. He would not be torn out of normalcy today. "Yeah, it's my normal pre-work routine."

She offered her hand to shake. "My name is Deb."

Deb. Deb. Deb. Sounded like a drug, he thought. Mainline some Deb. He shook her hand. It was soft. Softer than most girl hands he had touched. No calluses. No cuts. Just a soft, warm hand pressed against his. She smiled when he didn't let go in a reasonable amount of time. He smiled back. "I'm Kevin."

And then a dinner date.

At El Rancho, one of those Mexican restaurants that seemed to have zero Mexicans on staff. Deb lied to the waitress and said it was Kevin's birthday. The waitress brought out the rest of the staff, slapped a sombrero on his head and sang "Happy Birthday" before shoving a bowl of fried ice cream in front of him. He had never seen fried ice cream before. He couldn't even remember the last time he had eaten unfried ice cream. He went at it with his hands and Deb giggled, handing him a spoon. She showed him how to crack the shell and get a good spoonful of fried goodness along with the ice cream hidden within.

And then sex.

After their fourth date, she took him back to her place, a fancy apartment on the edge of downtown. She had vases. Art. She kiss-shoved him all the way to her bedroom and then pushed him onto the bed. She was still wearing her dress suit because they had met up right after work. It made her look powerful. So powerful.

"Punch me in the mouth," he said.

She screwed up her face and raised an eyebrow, but then made a fist and gently rapped her knuckles on his jaw, laughing.

Maybe normal people didn't do that when they fucked. He suddenly became super nervous, wondering what other stuff they didn't usually do. There was only one way to find out. He kicked off his slacks and waited.

Deb said nothing about the size of his penis. He knew it was small. Some girls liked to comment about it. They would say it was cute, or they would belittle him. Deb just dropped her skirt and lunged, face-first. She took it in her mouth and it went hard instantly. Then she climbed on. She rode him.

They maneuvered so he was on top. After she came, he squatted over her chest. He grunted, trying to squeeze a shit onto her boobs, but without his usual pre-fuck laxative, all he got was a turtlehead.

"What are you doing?" she asked, perhaps a little frightened.

That was all he needed to hear to know that shitting on a girl's tits post-sex wasn't the usual thing. "Just kidding," he said. He supposed that meant she wouldn't be shitting in his mouth either. Bummer.

Then he jerked off into her mouth and for some reason she was totally okay with that. Wasn't cum grosser than shit? He was going to have a hard time understanding normal versus abnormal when it came to sexy stuff, he realized. He decided to forego cutting open his scrote for now.

And then marriage.

They dated for nearly a year before he proposed. Although there was still part of him that just wanted to go on an endless fuck-spree, eating up every dick and pussy he could find, he was getting way into this monogamy thing. It was weird, having consistently good sex once or twice a day. It was exciting.

There was also an emotional connection. Deb would ask him questions he had never answered before, like "How was your day?" or "What are you thinking about?" or "What do you want the future to look like?" She seemed to legitimately care, and not in the way that his brother Merle had cared enough to pay for whores and heroin once in a while, but in a sort of normal way that he could barely understand and it made his heart race like he was on speed.

So he proposed and they got married in a small ceremony in Grant Park. He invited a couple co-workers who he had started hanging out with for football games and normal guy stuff, and she invited her sister and mom and a few friends. It was nice. It was so fucking nice.

And then kids.

They moved into Kevin's house, which had remained more or less unchanged since his arrival. Deb liked the exterior color, but required a fresh paint job. She bought a bunch of new furniture too. She made him throw out all the bedroom puppets. Turned out that was actually not super normal.

Deb vaj-blasted out kid number one within a year of tying the knot. It was a boy. A totally healthy and normal boy. Kevin and Deb agreed to name him Grant, after her deceased father who was a veteran. A year later came kid number two, a totally healthy and normal girl who they named Vanessa, because Deb thought that sounded like a model name and Vanessa was so pretty she was going to be a model for sure.

Kevin almost got derailed from normalcy watching Deb shove her milk-tits in the kids' mouths for them to slurp on, but he held it together.

He was good with the kids. He quit his job and became a stay-at-home dad, because Deb's salary was enough and the house was paid for, sort of. Grant's first word was "Daddy," which was about as normal as Kevin could have dreamed.

When they learned to walk, he played games with them in the backyard, trampling over the ground where the rotting corpses of the past homeowners were buried just a few feet deep. He played normal games with them, games like tag and soccer, games that didn't involve any measure of urine or blood. Actually, Vanessa fell and scraped her knee once, and not only did it bleed, but she got so worked up over the wound, she lost control of her bladder and piss shot out of her shorts. It was like old times, but Kevin did not smear any of the fluids on his face or his sex nub. He lovingly took Vanessa inside and washed her off. Grant watched, exclaiming how "Totawy gwoss and awesome" the mess was, because for some reason it's normal for young boys to be excited about that stuff, but not adults.

One sundrenched summer day when Grant was four and his Allin genes started to show through to the point of annoyance, he slapped Vanessa and dragged her by her hair across the backyard because she wouldn't let him play with one of her dolls. Kevin had become strangely protective of his brood, and it actually hurt him a little bit in the pit of his stomach to see either of them injured. The feeling was confusing as hell. One of those unforeseen excitements of normalcy. He tried hard to understand it, and kind of reveled in it. He sent Grant to the basement on time out, because he did that sort of thing now.

When time out was over, Grant emerged from the basement with a massive old garbage bag. Kevin had seen that bag before. He couldn't quite remember though. Had he killed a whore and put her, or him, in there before he had fully committed to normality? Shit, that would explain the smile on Grant's face.

"Daddy! Wook! Wook!" the kid exclaimed.

Vanessa fluttered around him like a butterfly, drawn to the excitement.

"I, uh, have never seen that bag before in my life," Kevin said, as if talking to police officers, although he had never said anything more than, "Fuck off you fucking pig cocksucker motherfuckers" to law enforcement before.

Grant reached into the bag, but instead of pulling out a severed slut limb, he retrieved a puppet – a nappy, blue-felt puppet with a burlap patch over its eye. Kevin remembered the puppets that had been in the bedroom. Deb had hated them. He wondered if she'd be pissed off that they got dragged out, but it made sense to Kevin to let the kids play with them. Shit, less money to spend on new toys.

"Oh yeah, my old puppet collection," he said, swiping One Eye from Grant. He looked closely at the puppet. It didn't look right. In it's one black eye, it held a lot of... He wanted to say hate. He wanted to say self-loathing. He wanted to say the stuff he used to see in his own eyes when he looked into the mirror, but that didn't make sense. This was a fucking puppet and that was a goddamn button, not an actual eye, and it couldn't hold emotion any more than the grass below his feet could.

He dropkicked it across the yard as Grant and Vanessa tore into the bag, pulling out dozens of ridiculous puppets. Grant shoved his hand into a furry red one wearing a tinsel boa around its fat neck. The boy held it up to Kevin and said, "This one wants to chew off your ears!"

Vanessa waved around a dragon puppet with a large, cotton-spewing gash across its belly. "This one wants to chew off your penis, Daddy!"

Kevin clenched his teeth. Where was this violent talk coming from all the sudden? He thought of the look in the one puppet's eye. Was it the puppets? Were they influencing the kids somehow? Ridiculous. These kids probably just really did have the Allin family genes. "Don't talk like that, kids. It's not normal."

Grant and Vanessa frowned in tandem for a second before giggling and going back to the business of sorting through the puppets. Kevin wondered why he hadn't thrown them away. Wait, hadn't he? Well, obviously not.

He left the kids to their mischief and went inside to make supper. Deb was celebrating her work anniversary, so he decided to cook his specialty: spicy sweet potato burritos. They burned so good coming out the back end. But that's not why he loved making them. He loved making them because they tasted delicious, and Deb agreed. And he had bought some brownies from the bakery down the street. It was going to be a really wonderful evening.

"My fingers got ated!" Grant screamed, crashing through the back door with blood spraying out of him as if it desperately needed to be someplace else, like the walls, the floor, all over Kevin's face.

Vanessa followed her brother, the dragon puppet clamped

to her shoulder and gnawing deep into her flesh. "Get it off, Daddy!"

Kevin tore the writhing puppet off his daughter. It was strong. He could feel the power of its jaws as they snapped at his face, but he managed to keep the teeth far enough away that he didn't lose his nose.

Cotton spewed out of its gut wound. It squirmed out of Kevin's hands, wrapped its long tail around his torso and squeezed. Kevin felt something. Was it a rib crack? It had been so long since he had felt pain so sweet. He moaned.

But now was not the time to revel in it. With his foot, he flipped the oven door open and threw the dragon puppet inside, onto the cookie sheet full of burritos, completely ruining them. He turned the oven up as hot as it would go. The puppet flapped its wings and collided with the element, catching fire.

Vanessa screeched.

Grant yelled, "Dad, they're coming!"

Kevin looked at the door. One of the puppets had made it inside. Legless, it propelled itself on thin, hollow arms. It looked at the family and cackled through a row of sharpened teeth. Kevin ran at it and kicked it back outside, where it landed on top of its cohorts, who crowd surfed it to the back of the pack. Kevin slammed the door shut, just as Deb entered through the front.

"I'm hoooo… oh my fucking god!" she screamed as she entered the kitchen and saw Grant's bleeding, fingerless hand. He still had his pinky bone, stripped of skin and outstretched daintily, but the rest were gone. Kevin took off his shirt and wrapped it around his son's bleeding mess.

"Puppets. Attacking. Now." That was all Kevin could think to say.

His heart beat so fast. Was it because of the excitement of having blood on his face again? He felt no urge to smear the crimson on his tattooed torso, to trace a bloodstained fingertip over the Live Fast Die logo that was once his motto, which he had now abandoned in favor of Live Slow Happy. No, his heart was beating so fast because he was in danger, because Deb was in danger, because the kids were in danger, because he cared about them. What the fuck?

Deb embraced him. His kids embraced them both. A family hug.

The puppets pounded on the back door. At first, it was cacophonous and undefined. Then it melted into a rhythm. Boom boom pow! Bang rap rap! Boom boom pow! Bang rap rap! And the puppets sang:

Violence now!
Fuck your corpse!
Brutality! Brutality!
Endless warrrrrrr!

Fuck. Were those his lyrics? Did the puppets know him? Did they know the real him. But this was the real him now: normal father and husband living in a nice house. Those weren't his words. They meant nothing to him. Only his family. These fuckers that had stolen his fucking heart. Fuck them. Let them die. No!

One Eye stared in through the kitchen window, gnawing the head off a squirrel. It used the blood as lube to masturbate a little felt nub that bulged above its puppet hole. It came fast, shooting a neon pink load all over the glass. It smeared cum and squirrel blood on the window, and then, with its now flaccid puppet dong, wrote the word "Kill."

In a voice like a derailing train, One Eye bellowed, "I'm gonna fuck your fat dead ass. I'm gonna fuck your whole family after I kill them and suck out the goodies from their stomachs!"

Kevin could picture this happening. And he was scared.

Then he thought, why the fuck am I scared? I'm fucking GG Allin!

Except he wasn't. Not anymore.

"Kevin, you have to stop them!" Deb pleaded.

169

But he wasn't a person who could stop them. He had grown pudgy. He had gotten weak. He was a normal, family man, and one thing a normal family man didn't do was fight off packs of cock- and cunt-hungry puppets.

"I'll call the police," he said, reaching for the phone.

"The police? Kevin, there are dozens of those things. They are going to be in here any second now, and they are going to hurt us. You need to stop them."

"I am a normal man," he whined.

"You have to protect your family!" Deb screamed.

He curled his hands into fists. He looked at his scarred knuckles. He could do it. He could open up the floodgates and let GG Allin take over, but then what? GG Allin was powerful. Kevin was not. And Kevin liked this life. It was so sublimely normal, so comfortable. He could live this life forever. Surely the police would be here in time. This was Chicago, after all.

He undid his fists and reached for the phone.

He typed in 911.

He didn't even get past the first ring before the backdoor exploded under the weight of the encroaching puppets. The biggest one led the way, a goat-horned beast with purple fur so tangled it seemed like it was strangling itself, an impression furthered by the way its black tongue dangled from its wide mouth. This puppet had legs, and it moved quickly on them, quickly toward Kevin's family.

It drove its left horn into Vanessa's stomach, ripping through her shirt, ripping through her. She cried out, hands reaching for her mother. A flank of meat hung by her side, where the horn had exited. A little shard of rib jutted out, like a horn of her own. Blood poured out like tar. She lost the strength of her legs, but Deb held her up. Vanessa's eyelids fluttered closed.

Goat Horns clamped down on Deb's leg, but Deb kicked it off and stomped on it. It seemed impervious to stomping. Just plush and stuffing. There was nothing to break. Nothing to damage. One of its eyeballs popped off and it laughed.

"I'm going to eat your womb, bitch," Goat Horns said as Deb stomped.

A cape-wearing, flesh-colored puppet with a black mask and a plastic pompadour flew at Grant. With surprisingly nimble fingers, it unwrapped the T-shirt from the boy's wound and then wrapped it's mouth around the mutilated hand, slurping up the blood as its massive eyeballs rolled back in ecstasy.

Deb swatted it away. She lifted the two kids off the ground. She kicked and stomped at the army of puppets. She glared at Kevin, who merely stood on the other side of the kitchen, sweating and crying. "Please," she begged.

And he realized he had no choice. His family would die if he didn't help them. They would die and he would die too. But he wanted to die on his own terms. Ideally by his own hand. And while drunk and high. Not by killer fucking puppets.

He spread his arms wide and roared. With both fists, he punched himself in the face, again and again. The old wounds opened up fast, remembering this. Blood poured from his forehead, from his nose. He saw red. He legitimately saw red. The blood framed his vision.

"What are you...? Kevin?" Deb asked, out of breath from the fight.

"I'm not Kevin," he said as he snatched up the already somewhat mangled body of Goat Horns. He bit into its face and tore off a hunk of plush, which he immediately spit to the floor. "I'm GG fucking Allin."

He took another bite. Oily muck oozed out of the puppet's wounds. It tasted like black licorice on GG's tongue. He smiled and it dribbled from the corners of his mouth. He threw the now-limp puppet aside and caught another one, the superhero blood-slurper. He wrapped its cape around its neck, tighter and tighter, until its head popped off and black goo drained from its neck.

GG's cock got hard.

He didn't toss the headless puppet away. Instead, he dropped his slacks and impaled his dick in the inky stump,

171

swabbing his member around inside the still-twitching puppet as the other puppets watched on, suddenly not so tough. He pumped and pumped and quickly ejaculated, so hard his white slime shot out through the thing's empty puppet hole.

Deb gasped. She covered Grant's eyes. Vanessa was passed out from the severity of her wound. Deb said, "Kevin, just… just kill them normal?"

"I'm not normal!" he yelled as he grabbed two more puppets by their heads and tore them asunder with his hands, hands already so soaked in cum and blood that they were starting to look familiar, they were starting to look like his hands.

Realizing they had much more of a challenge than they had anticipated, the puppets worked together now. They charged at GG, bearing claws, bearing teeth, bearing horns. GG kicked and punched.

An anus-faced puppet latched onto GG's nipple with little pin-like teeth. Oh, but it felt good. He got hard again as blood poured from his chest wound like electricity, lighting him up. Ripping the puppet free, he got an idea.

He took a squat and, as if all his repressed bowel muscle memory suddenly overcame the self-induced amnesia, he shot a stream of feces so wet and fast it splattered off the kitchen tile and gave his backside an upside down shit shower. He scooped up handfuls and smeared them over the eyes of every puppet he could reach, blinding them and slowing them down enough to give him time to properly execute each and every one of them, which he did, as his wife watched.

When he was done, he stood, breathing heavy, ankle deep in scrap material and black puppet guts. He couldn't keep his hand off his cock.

"Kevin? I don't understand. What are you doing?" Deb asked, as if he was the bad guy, as if he had threatened to kill the family. Well maybe his family deserved to fucking die. Maybe everyone deserved to fucking die.

Before he could address that, Deb pointed to the kitchen window.

That blue-faced, one-eyed fucker was still there, sneering.

GG punched through the glass and grabbed the final puppet by its neck. He squeezed the thing's head, mushing it up and covering it with slick bodily fluids, lubing it up for easy entry. Then he jammed the puppet headfirst up his ass. Groaning, he worked it in and out, using two hands at first, before freeing one up so he could jerk his nub. He realized his wife was still watching.

"Suck my cock," he ordered.

"Wh-what?" she asked.

"Suck my fucking cock, now!"

GG stepped toward her and grabbed her by the back of her head, getting a solid grip on her soft blonde hair. He pushed her to her knees.

Grant dragged his sister to the far side of the kitchen as she blinked back into consciousness. She would die soon. Maybe Grant would too. Who could tell how the rest of the day might go?

The sound of sirens answered that question. The 911 call must have gone through. They must have traced it. Just like the fucking pigs. Too late to help, but just in time to fuck up the party.

They smashed down the front door and charged into the kitchen. Four barrel-chested boys in blue, ready to inflict the law on somebody.

GG tossed his wife aside and threw shit at the pigs.

They were on him fast. He couldn't stop them. They took him down. They cuffed him. They dragged him away in a headlock. Deb ran behind, angry now, but not at the cops. "What's wrong with you?" she screeched.

"This world is what's wrong with me. This fucking world and everything in it. I hate you! You hear me? I love nothing. I love no one. I hate everyone and everything, and I always fucking will, forever and ever until the end of fucking time!"

And then the cops pulled out their nightsticks.

FUCK THE UNIVERSE

Sam Richard

Nineteen-ninety-three. Fuck. Nineteen and fucking ninety-three, since we last spoke. Jesus. Here I've gone and lived what should have been an entire lifetime, twenty-two years worth at least, and you're still fucking laying there, tube down your throat, those fucking IV drips keeping you balanced and fed, pissing and shitting into a bag, in this fucking coma ward, the smells of mouse shit and disinfectant battling for nasal supremacy. And you just keep fucking sleeping – Aaron, you stupid fuck. I'd like to think that you'd have found this funny, had you known where we'd end – where you'd end.

I can so vividly recall that night. It's scary to think that it was that fucking long ago. You and Jim and I crammed into that awful Olive colored Pinto, with the interior an alternate gross color of light green, that Mom gave you when she bought her new car. Years prior, it was supposed to be recalled, what with the back-end on those things lighting up like a match when kissed with the lightest, feather-touch of rear impact. But she kept it, and you kept fucking driving it.

The three of us, some sleeping-bags, a stolen carton of Pall-Mall, a case of cheap swill, maybe a cheese-crusted burger wrapper or two, and about $15 between us? Jesus, a few dumb fucking kids, trying to have a night – a week? a life? – on the town. Driving from Maine to fucking Manhattan, like a group of goddamn assholes, to see a fucking show you just wouldn't shut up about for weeks. Fuck. Sometimes, I really hate you, Aaron. I always thought that in the end, you'd pull me into some straight-up crazy ass bullshit, but I figured I'd be the one who paid the price for it. And I suppose I am, in my own twisted way.

All that, just to end up here, to end up…wherever the

hell you are in there. What did you call him? "The punching, shitting King of Scum?" Fucking Christ, with all your book smarts, and you still fall head-over-heels for some poorly done shock-parlor act. Fuck you. Doesn't matter. After tonight I'm done fucking crying about this. No more searching, no more back-alley deals, no more money spent, no more emotional drain. One last shot, then I have to live my fucking life for me, what's left of it. This has cost me too much; it cost us all.

Did I tell you what Jim's last words to me were? He called me up: "Kate, I think I found it! This guy I met at Vendetta told me he had a line on what we're looking for. This has to be it." My heart felt like it was going to punch through my rib cage, I remember my knees going a little weak. "Tell me when and where. I'll meet you. I've got some money." He was silent for an eerie amount of time, then meekly spoke. "It's too late. I bought it. I already took it. Supposed to be his blood. I'll get Aaron back." And the line went dead. I rushed out of the apartment, praying that Jim had called me from home. Before I even got to his door I could smell it. Hot and sickly, that rancid cancer-sweat smell clouded the floor of his building like sarin gas in the still desert.

I didn't want to open the door; I already knew what was inside. Reluctantly, I pushed in and found an indecipherable pile of bones and skin resting atop a steaming puddle of blue. Pale slime dotted the walls and ceiling, burning little holes in the gaudy 70's wallpaper. His clothing, carpet, hair, and shoes appeared to be dripping through the floorboards, like escape was their only option. I didn't yell, I didn't cry, I didn't stop to look for any clues. He was gone, and that was one more dead fucking end in a lifetime of dead ends.

Later, I found the guy who sold him what was alleged to be GG's blood. After threatening to tear out his windpipe with a rusty screwdriver he came clean. Turned out it was Merle's blood. And, as it happens, Merle's blood is like sulfuric acid mixed with demon cum. Basically, it dissolved Jim's innards and left him a stinking pile of goo. Eventually we'll all end up a pile of rot and confusion. He just did it a lot more quickly.

But the show that fucking night, my god I don't think I'd ever seen a man possessed by so much blind self-hatred in my entire life. Don't get me wrong, his hatred for the audience was insane and intriguingly frightening, but it was rivaled by how much that man hated himself, that night at least.

I remember that we arrived late and missed the opening bands. We just kept drinking with the hatch open on the car. You were half dazed from the trip down, half-electrified by the idea of seeing the show. I was just tired and slightly annoyed, at least until I had a few. I couldn't tell you why I agreed to come to the show; maybe I wanted to see the spectacle as badly as you did? Maybe I've reinvented my position on the whole thing and now I want to be morally separate from it. Maybe, at the time, I was just as excited for his madness. Sometimes, Aaron, it's just so easy to blame you for all of this.

We wandered into the club, right? Slightly drunk, and there's just shouting going on. The band is on the floor, sort of fiddling around with their instruments, but nothing is coming out of the PA, and GG is standing on stage yelling at the sound guy, who's yelling back. Just a barrage of insults only slightly audible above the restless crowd, who are also screaming at the sound guy, like walking into an asylum about to be overrun by the charismatic leader of the inmates; a Weissian de Sade at Charenton Asylum. As we grabbed some drinks and continued to watch, I couldn't help but wonder if this was part of the show? Eventually, someone comes out with a microphone and GG plugs it in and the band starts playing.

The awkwardness from when we first showed up only continued, as the band struggled to keep playing as GG alternated between yelling, rolling on the ground, assaulting the audience, kicking the drum-set and leaving the venue, microphone still in hand. What was supposed to be this great maelstrom of chaotic energy really felt like the end of something greater, something we missed completely. Sure, it's easy to say those words in hindsight, but at the time I really felt like we were catching the tail end of something that would have meant more to us had we been there from the start. This sermon was not for us, it was for the true believers, the dedicated who read the signs and knew what was next, so many things lost in translation that it couldn't have the sort of impact on us that I now know it needed to have. Like only reading the last chapter of a book, it was ultimately lost on us. There was no glossary of terms, no map-key for what was going on.

Like all his major ceremonies that had come before, this ended in blood, it ended in shit, it ended in bile, it ended in derangement of the senses, it ended in religious fervor; and it ended in death, it ended in revelation, it ended in – what I believe to be – the birth of a new world. It took you from me, but in doing so it opened my eyes to what lies beyond the wall of sleep. This place we are now is not where you truly rest, and I am coming to meet you. We are going to be together, in paradise.

From there, everything gets a little blurry, like getting punched in the mouth repeatedly with a massive fist of bad acid. The violence climaxed and the taste of blood, sweat, and shit assaulted my senses. GG's lumbering body collided into me and I fell to the floor. The feeling of GG feces in my eye is one thing that, despite trying, I will never be able to forget. As he shit into his hand, just inches from me, I remember – once again – being furious with you. This feeling quickly turned to joy as he smashed his freshly laid log right into your face. And then he just kept rubbing it, and rubbing it, and rubbing it, and smashing it until you were bleeding from your nose and coughing up the feces that had made it into your sinuses and down your throat. As he pushed you down, a truly wild and feral look in his eyes, he leaned back down to me and said, "This is my body, broken for you."

A wave of euphoria took over and my spine shuddered like the temperature in the room had just dropped 50 degrees. I got up and came to you but you were out like it was the days of Pentecost and tongues of fire had descended upon us. Your lips were moving but you were inaudible. Jim pushed past the surging audience and helped me pick you up. As we headed through the mass of bodies the room started to pulse and the walls breathed in and out. By the time we got outside I had dropped you, leaving Jim to carry you himself, and I stumbled in the general direction of the car, but that street in Manhattan no longer looked how it had when we arrived there. I looked up. Structures defying the laws of physics jutted out from the ground and seemed to wrap around each other, constantly shifting and creating new clusters with shapes that made no logical sense. They were set back against a pale green sky filled with cosmic fractals and shapes shooting off into unidentifiable dimensions.

As I looked down at what had once been the road, everything seemed to converge at a center mass. These shifting structures breathed together in an eerie motion, constantly pushing and pulling as if part of one unified organism. The monolith at the center, set apart from everything else, as though an invisible barrier held the tendrils back, towered over all else in the landscape motionless. The horror of what I was seeing made my mind go strangely calm and Zen like.

The shadow the monstrosity cast blotted out the three major cosmic sources of light. I tried to head away from the monstrosity, but every direction I went somehow, and beyond reason, would direct me back towards the center of the slumbering obelisk. As my confusion became unbearable, I began to run. Away from, no towards, but then away from and yet towards, once again, the central structure.

With no other option, I walked towards the center. The closer I got, the more the smaller bodies, mirroring the large writhing structures above, littered the path in front of me. They were plantlike and moved in a different, yet also unified, fashion. Eventually, there were so many that the path basically vanished. I tried to walk upon them but in doing so I tripped and fell into the pile. As soon as I hit the ground, these plants tried to grab hold of me. I struggled to break free from their grip, but I shockingly found myself no longer confined by the plants, or surrounded by writhing bodies, but rather laying on the sidewalk, a few cars down from the Pinto.

Jim had placed you in the backseat and came to help me up. He said that I had been screaming incoherently and running around like a mad woman. Surprised by my sudden lucidity, he insisted that we rush you to a hospital. I got into the car and struggled into the tiny back seat next to you.

My muscles were on fire and I felt a Dionysian hangover approaching. I held you, calling you back to me, crying for you to wake up. I knew that this was in vain. I knew then what I know now: you are in that place. For 22 years, you've been trapped in that labyrinth and for 22 years, I haven't been able to help you. Then we brought you to the hospital. And things have remained this way. That ends tonight.

I came here because I found it. After all these failures, after Jim's death, after injecting and snorting and huffing and digesting everything from Dino's dried semen to Chicken John's snot to Dee Dee's piss to probably the shit, vomit, and blood of hobos and junkies and scam artists alike, I've fucking found it.

Thanks to luck or god or Satan or gods older than time, I was able to track down the janitor of the Gas Station who worked the night of that show. After the maelstrom and chaos and violence of that night, he went to work cleaning. He ended up accidentally flicking some vomit on his cheek as he took his gloves off. While much shorter than what happened to me, he described in insane detail a very similar experience. He knew this was important, so he gathered up as much of what GG left behind as possible and freeze-dried it until he could figure out what to do with it. Having about as much luck as I did with finding anyone who knew what was going on with this, he decided to store it in safety until he could find a lead.

Years went by, but he eventually figured that he could at least make a buck by selling the stuff as psychedelic substances. At first, he only made a few sales, because people didn't know what it was he was selling. See the guy isn't that bright, but eventually he came up with some chemistry name for it – GG628, very creative, right – and it took off in the boutique drug market. I found him through The Silk Road. Wow, wait. You don't know what the Internet is. Weird. Well anyhow, the description he gives, as well as the reviews, are exactly what happened to me.

He warned me not to take too much, because people have been known to have memory loss from too much and go into comas if they take a fuck-ton. This has to be it. I bought all that I could. He typically puts it in small capsules, but I bought a big vial of the stuff. I'm taking it, now. Aaron, I'm coming for you.

☻☻☻

Through eyes not my own – dark, pupil-less eyes staring from behind mine – I bare witness to her arrival. She will see the me that is not me. She will believe the illusion and there is nothing I can do but watch. For years, I have heard her voice in my head and listened as she struggled to make sense of what has happened to me. This whole time, I've known today would eventually arrive and He did too. He wanted this. He needs her, and he needs my body, which he took so long ago, to open the doorway back home, and to bring this all back with Him.

As We approach her, I struggle to fight against His possession, but I am resigned to failure. He is too strong, He controls us all and He will not be stopped. I notice, through Our eyes, the others, creeping up behind her as she runs to greet Us. Wild eyed with tears streaming down her cheeks, this would be the best day of my life if it wasn't the worst in a lifetime of horrendous days.

I wish I could convey what it has been like here. I wish there was anyone who could hear these thoughts and understand what is about to happen. Time has no meaning, space has no logic, and the universe will mean nothing as soon as this grotesque show finally comes to a halt. Amidst all the blood,

180

shit, semen, and pain there will be space for little else. I now understand His human form had to die, but He didn't understand how difficult it would be to get back to our world with his unified Self.

These other people here, much like me, are mere tourists – those who accidentally stumbled, or were pushed, here by accident. There are True Believers among us, but I've scarcely seen them, only their great works. Like her, they came here willingly. They came because something called them over. Unlike her, the True Believers made conditions right, both on this side – beyond space and time – and back home for His immortal reign. I'm sure they'll be the first to find the comfort of void in blood. Unlike her, they knew what they were getting into. She didn't. He needs willingness. He also needs ignorance.

It hurts to watch, but I know what is going to come next. I scratch and punch and scream but nothing and no one can hear me. This is agony. As she gets close enough to touch, and they grab her. We open Our robes to reveal this twisted, mutilated body and unsheathe the Obsidian Ritual knife. The joy and shock on her face don't waiver, as though she can't be bothered to understand what is about to happen to her, despite the knife and the hands pulling at her, I'm sure Our face doesn't betray how I feel. We're all just too happy to see each other.

And then blood, and a piercing shriek cut short and muffled by one sob. It is done. Her body rises up, the wound splitting her flesh and tearing at the fabric of space and time. Winds from nowhere whip past and I can smell the sickly-sweet scent of decay as the monolith ascends to meet the portal, now massive and covered in purple goo. The wind pulls everyone towards the portal and We're swept up amongst the debris. My body matters not, for He has many, and we're all just pawns.

I reach the Monolith as it enters the Portal and Our legs are pulled into the swirling vortex. The Monolith pushes in and I become wedged between the fleshy rim and the rigid Obelisk. It is at this moment, as Our body finally breaks between Monolith and Void, that I understand everything.

SPECIAL SCUMFUC THANKS TO
JOHN PHILLIPS II

Special thanks to these sexy perverts who backed the Kickstarter and helped make this madness possible:

Teresa Pollack
Warren "Nasty" Mastronardi
Viktor Tavarez
Nick Johnson
Mo Richard
Stephan Imri-Knight
John Wayne Comunale
Rev. Eryk Pruitt
Christian Hanson
Joe Miller
Paul Anderson
Don't Damn the Torpedos,
    just shoot Lloyd and Alicia
Glenn Stanley
Gerisati George
Stephen Malt Laxton
Scott Cole
John Bruni
William Tea
Joel D. Kaplan
Mary Farrell
Charlie Litz
Brandon Stroth
Josh Spicoli Martens
T. K. Spragg Chad Bowden
Scott "The Rudeboy" Ruud
Robin Lantz
Aaron M. Wilson

Tanner Ballengee
Rodney Gardner
Chris Mihal
Derek Ailes
Michael Barrett
Chad Reeves
Brandon Wright
Erika Instead
Joe D Peterson
Scott Kirkland
Rick Westbrock
Garageadelic Joanis
Travis Phillips
Lasergoon
Josh Vanderloop
Rev. Michael C. Manning
Livius Nedin
Sasha D
MWdaag
Frank Edler
Cody Mohler
Christoph Paul
Jeffrey Jones
Michelle Garza
T.A. Wardrope
Sue See
Justin Hunter

EDITOR BIOS

MP JOHNSON spent his high school lunch hours in the library listening to tapes on his walkman. Once he let some other kid listen to his Hated in the Nation tape. MP was like, "Isn't this sick?" The other kid was all, "That's not the sickest shit I've ever heard." And then they got in a fistfight after school. MP's short stories have appeared in more than 50 publications. His debut book, The After-Life Story of Pork Knuckles Malone, was a Wonderland Book Award finalist. His most recent books include Dungeons and Drag Queens, Cattle Cult! Kill! Kill! and Sick Pack. He is the creator of Freak Tension zine, a B-movie extra, an amateur drag queen and an obsessive music fan currently based in Minneapolis. Learn more at www.freaktension.com.

SAM RICHARD may be the only person in this anthology who isn't actually a fan of GG Allin, outside of a morbid fascination. That's OK though, because he likes all sorts of other fucked up stuff, which is probably why MP asked him to co-edit Blood For You. Previously bassist in the Crust band War//Plague, he now plays Black Metal guitar in Daoloth and has written for many publications including Profane Existence, Cvlt Nation, The Pulse, and No//Vanguard. He is currently, and slowly, working on several transgressive and vile book projects that may see the light of day, eventually. More at: amotherfuckingwerewolf.tumblr.com and @SammyTotep on Twitter

AUTHOR BIOS

ANDREW WAYNE ADAMS is the author of Janitor of Planet Anilingus (a bizarro novella) and numerous short stories that have appeared throughout the ages both in print and online. His mom bought him a GG Allin CD for Christmas once, and he's been a fan ever since.

RICHARD ARNOLD is not a writer, but does co-host The Fifth Dimension Podcast, and used to write a shitty, boring zine a long time ago. He is fairly bladder-shy, so more than anything he finds GG Allin impressive for his ability to defecate while even one other person is watching, much less a whole audience. He currently resides in Minneapolis, MN.

JOHN BRUNI, author of Poor Bastards and Rich Fucks and Tales of Questionable Taste, came to the party late in life. He fell in love with GG Allin long after his death when he saw Chad Ginsburg drunkenly pissing on his hero's grave. As soon as John learned the significance of this, he hunted down GG's work, his favorite being "Die When You Die." John lives and fucks and shits in Elmhurst, IL.

JEFF BURK is the cult favorite author of Shatnerquake, Super Giant Monster Time, Cripple Wolf, and Shatnerquest. Like the literary equivalent to a cult B-Horror movie, Burk writes violent, absurd, and funny stories about punks, monsters, gore, and trash culture. Everyone normally dies at the end. He was once told that he looked like GG Allin – he still isn't sure if that was a compliment or an insult.

NICK CATO is the author of one novel, five novellas, and one short story collection, as well as a forthcoming book on grind-house cinema. In 1985, Nick's friend John Lisa let him borrow a 7" record titled GG Allin and the Scumfucs and he has been a fan ever since. In 1986, Nick and John survived GG Allin and the NY Super Scum at the Cat Club in NYC, considered by GG himself as being the "Second sickest gig I ever did." Nick's favorite GG song is "Don't Talk to Me." You can find Nick on the usual sites as well as nickyakcato.blogspot.com.

NICHOLAS DAY discovered GG Allin through Kenny Joslen, who was as punk-as-fuck when they were kids and remains so to this day. GG didn't give a shit, and Nicholas wrote a story to reflect that. If he could crawl out of this book and shit in your lap, well, he would love to, but you'll have to settle for his words. Nicholas's novella Necrosaurus Rex is available through Bizarro Pulp Press. Recent short stories have been published through the likes of JEA Wetworks, James Ward Kirk Fiction, Morpheus Tales, and Pro Se Productions. He owns a poodle named Murder Princess.

DAVID C. HAYES is the author of bizarro/horror/splatter like Cherub and The Midnight Creature Feature Picture Show. His films, like Back Woods, Dark Places and Bloody Bloody Bible Camp can be seen worldwide. That doesn't matter. What matters is that he discovered GG Allin a little too late in life. In college, 1991, and a random episode of Geraldo. The man that said his body was a temple to rock and roll fascinated the frustrated writer, stuck in a place that did not appreciate the bizarre and extreme. Thus, a lifelong love/hate relationship with the performer developed and, unable to see him play live, David made do with the Phillips documentary and the music. The ability to eulogize Allin, even at this late date, is a precious thing to him and he hopes his story is a fitting homage.

You hate GABINO IGLESIAS and he hates you. No one ever understands the things he says or does, so what's new? You never liked him so he says fuck everything and writes. He's sad that he found San GG so late in life and only met folks who shared his love for him even later. He wrote Gutmouth, Hungry Darkness, Zero Saints, and this, among other things. Who wants a hug?

JOEL KAPLAN drinks, fights, and fucks in Sarasota, Florida. He bled out the extreme cult horror novel High on Blood at the End of the World. He is originally from Maine where GG recorded his first album. His favorite tune is "Highest Power" because he agrees that Jesus Christ was a son of a bitch. He once accidentally ate way too much cough medicine with Jack Acid and they embarked on a spontaneous yet successful midnight pilgrimage to visit GG's grave. He could kick your ass at pinball. Send your skulls to joeldkaplan@hotmail.com or @maxreverb666 on twitter.

SHAWN MILAZZO has written for BizarroCentral.com's Flash Fiction Friday, The Horror Press, and WitchWorks Pulp Horror Magazine to name a few. My Shadow's Footsteps, a crime horror comic landed him a membership to the Horror Writers Association. Living in Toledo, Ohio, Shawn remembers seeing GG Allin on television during GG's 1989 trial. Being a fan of politics, free speech, rebelliousness, art and noise, Shawn branched out to underground genres of music during the 90's. His favorite GG Allin song is "When I Die." Shawn is currently working on his erotica horror novella titled: Pounded by Pod People.

JORGE PALACIOS is an author and zinester from the post-apocalyptic wasteland known as Puerto Rico, specializing in horror and porn. His influences are punk rock and beer. He first heard of GG Allin when he saw the documentary Hated as a teenager; he didn't know if GG was a noncomformist genius, or a degenerate scumbag (both definitions apply). "Don't Talk To Me" is his favorite song.

NICHOLAUS PATNAUDE grew up in Connecticut. After completing his degree at Bard College, he worked abroad in Turkey and Bolivia. His illustrated novel, First Aide Medicine, won the 2010 International Emergency Press contest and was published on June 4th, 2013. He currently lives and works in Virginia. He can be found blogging about underground writers, psychedelic music, and cult cinema at nicholauspatnaude.com or on twitter at @poemcultureblog. His favorite GG Allin song is "Bite It, You Scum." He first encountered infamous tales of GG Allin's tyrannical assault on good taste in the newsprint pages of MaximumRocknRoll and Flipside during the late 90s; once he procured some scratched Allin 45s, he became fascinated with the man, the music, the myths, and the flawed legends.

AIRIKA SNEVE is a writer, musician, and University of MN graduate from Minnesota. She enjoys ham, cats, and urinary alliteration by the master of punk prose, GG Allin (in particular "Sleeping in My Piss"). Her work has been published by Pill Hill Press, Crowded Quarantine Publications, Horrified Press, Issue #3 of Nameless Magazine, Strange Musings Press, and StrangeHouse Books.

KEVIN STRANGE is a two-time nominee for the Wonderland book award for excellence in bizarro fiction. He first discovered GG Allin in the cult movie shelf at his local mom and pop video store back when those were things that existed. He rented Hated: GG Allin and the Murder Junkies just because it looked fucked up. Then he rented it again to show his friends, and finally just stole the VHS copy because that's how you pirated movies back in those days. "You Hate Me and I Hate You" and "Don't Talk to Me" were the soundtrack to his life for many years to come, leading to that worn out "Fuck You" face that he walks around with today

ARTIST BIOS

JUSTIN T. COONS is a freelance artist and illustrator who works in the traditional mediums of paint and ink. He specializes in neo-pulp, horror, bizarro, and pinup artwork. Justin is a big fan of the Carnival of Excess album and respecting authority. GG does not approve.

CORY HANCOCK's favorite GG Allin song is "I Wanna Fuck Myself." Cory has been a professional horror artist since age seventeen and has been featured in prestigious gallery showings at The Brass Bell, Tall Hill Collective, and Tree & Leaf. He attends local Oklahoma City events, as well as being the art director for movie poster art and nationally featured commercials. Find other works of art by Cory at http://coryhancockart. deviantart.com/.

DAN WIEKEN considers GG's music to be wonderfully atrocious, yet identifies the man as the most wonderful freak show atrocity, for artistic rendering. Fitting into an artistic niche, including punk and metal shirt and album art, and a metal logo book and porno gag comic from Uncivilized Books. He also plays in the blackened doom post metal band Blood Folke.

Made in the USA
Charleston, SC
14 October 2015